A TOUCH OF
STRANGE

ADAM-TROY CASTRO

A tip of the hat to—

Stephen King
Theodore Sturgeon
Shirley Jackson
Donald Westlake

—and the rest of the Good Guys.

TABLE OF CONTENTS

INTRODUCTION:
BEYOND THE REACH
OF HUMAN RANGE...

This is a collection of some of my stranger, harder-to-classify recent short fiction.

Some of you must always know if any of it is infected with horror cooties. Well, yes; you can tell that some of it comes from the same basic neighborhood. But no, carnage of any kind is not the focus here. With these stories I was deliberately starting in strange places and seeing where the journey took me. If you want the genuinely horror-tinged, you would probably best-served in seeking out my 2012 collection, *Her Husband's Hands And Other Stories*, though stories of the sort are always lurking around whenever the tide brings more than a few of my tales between covers.

Still, the focus here is the strange.

"One Wild Night" is somewhere between horror and science fiction and an action-packed rumination on the nasty shit women have to deal with, albeit one ultimately triumphant for my protagonist, a successful woman who was once an actress and finds out here that the skills are still helpful against technology known as TIM. It bounced around for close for ten years before finally seeing print in the new iteration of *Pulphouse* Magazine, issue 19.

"The Monkey Trap" also tips to horror, but to me the key to the story is its portrait of a very strange bookstore where I would browse forever but hate to find one of my own volumes. It was published in *Nightmare* magazine, October 2020.

"The Last to Matter" was a story I worked on for almost twenty years and my secret attempt to complete the diptych begun by Robert Bloch's "A Toy For Juliette" and Harlan Ellison's "The Prowler in the City at the Edge of the World." As far as I am concerned, it is the third story in that trilogy. I cannot say so officially, but "as far as I am concerned" covers a lot of ground. Published in *Lightspeed* Magazine, September 2018.

"Sand Castles" is a Serlingesque tale based on the premise that the universe has issues of scale and that this means that we are all lumbering monsters to somebody, even if we're just decaying old barflies long soused out of our senses of wonder. From the July 2019 *Lightspeed*.

"Blood Relations," the most easily classifiable story of this bunch, is a dark look of the places where it looks like this country is heading, and a visit with three women who survive to emerge from the shadows. It is a hopeful if angry piece of work, and, I think, one of my five all-time best. It appeared in an anthology called *Or Else The Light*, in 2020.

"Cards on the Table," found a home shortly before I found out that someone had put together a collection paying tribute to the great Shirley Jackson. I had no problem with *Pulphouse*, that took it, but I confess regret. Because this story is Shirley Jackson if nothing else I've ever written is. Appeared in *Pulphouse* issue 18.

"The End of the World, Measured in Values of *N*," is a deceptively short piece that summarizes my current bleak feelings about the state of the world. First published in *Lightspeed*, June 2020.

"In the Temple of Celestial Pleasures" is an Asian-accented story, one of three I did in rapid succession. I have largely avoided outright horror in this compilation, which is why you're not getting, among other things, "James in the Golden Sunlight of the Hereafter." However, this one goes to some cringey places that resulted in its publication in a horror venue, and so I offer a content warning to the sensitive. Here there are triggers. First Published in *Nightmare*, May 2014.

"A Tableau of Things that Are" is a love story that ends, I think, with one of the best closing images I have ever stumbled on. It appeared in *Lightspeed*, June 2021.

And so, this is my collection of the unclassifiable. I hope you enjoy. Thanks to Glenn Hauman, John Joseph Adams, and Dean Wesley Smith.

—Adam-Troy Castro

ONE WILD NIGHT

Sunny was just high enough to overlook Pierce being too drunk to drive, and far too horny to care that she'd have a hell of a time retrieving her Prius if she was silly enough to leave the party in his blood-red Ferrari.

Casual hookups weren't her usual thing, but for whatever reason mysterious to her at the time, either the inexplicable powerful chemistry that can erupt between two strangers or the specific portion of that chemistry that she'd already altered with punch, practicality and common sense had flown out her ears the instant she'd met this guy normally so very not her type. She joined his flight from the party long before his boss Steve could get around to boring everybody with his speech about the new media paradigm.

Everybody knew the speech was coming, as Whizzards was already well on its way to becoming the new Industrial Light and Magic even before the whispers started about their new tech, but who the hell needed to politely applaud self-congratulation from the CEO when there was frenzied fucking to be done, somewhere out there in the night? Pierce confided, "I wrote the damn speech anyway," and she rewarded this with giggles more fervent than the minor revelation required.

The odd and wonderful and baffling thing for her was: they were *sincere* giggles.

Sunny -- and yes, that was her real name; thank you so very goddam much, Mom and Dad -- didn't have the slightest idea what the hell it was about Pierce, one of Whizzard's prime movers, maybe second or third in command under the *Time* cover boy Steverino. But whatever drew her to him sure as hell wasn't about the inherent sex appeal of his firm's contribution to the hit movie about the civil war between the mops and the brooms. It wasn't even his looks, which were young and chiseled and tanned but hardly out of the ordinary in this town where so many young men aspired to be James Dean by way of the greek gods.

The truth was she hadn't felt this giddy and impulsive, so *girlish*, since her own acting days, now more than a decade in the past. And that was saying a lot, because what a flighty girly-girl she'd been back then; getting so bored stiff in her freshman year of college that she'd sold the books and hitched out to LA *before* telling her parents that this was what she'd decided to do (on the quite sensible theory that they would have done everything short of a deprogramming session to stop her). That little life transition had been followed by five years of what she now called her silly-twat era having far more success in the thespic line than 99% of the beautiful leggy blondes who came out to this land of swimming pools and wild fires, which is to say *not quite* zero: a grand total of six national commercials, four two-liners, her biggest role involving a memorable on-screen death as the murdered girlfriend an action hero had to slaughter half of Central America in order to avenge, followed by one or two other little things of lesser consequence; and finally once coming *this* (fingers held one wry inch apart), *this* goddammit *this* close to getting the break-out role that at the last minute went to some other silly quiff who now seemed to have built a permanent condominium on the Oscar short list.

No, not *quite* zero. But by Sunny's lights it had never quite progressed beyond *almost* nothing, and while it was possible that if she'd stuck it out another year or two she'd have been Jessica Chastain now, she'd ultimately given herself a hard look at the mirror and said, damn it, girl, if you don't watch out you're going to end up remembered instead as no more than this decade's Joy Bang (look it up). So she'd retreated. Six subsequent months of serving as personal assistant to a perfectly nice elderly movie icon of gradually diminishing capacity and she'd found herself looking in the mirror again and this time saying, damn it, girl, you don't want to be remembered as this generation's Erin Fleming either (look *that* up). So what with one thing or another and a couple of additional false starts and angry hang-up endings to the inevitable I-Told-You-So phone conversations from Mom, she'd found a safe landing space in a costume design firm and was now a decade later Vice-President of the damn place, making a very nice living thank you, and the splendid irony of the thing was that she'd have a piece of an Oscar sooner or later while the girl who beat her out all those years ago was Lohanning her way through the tabloids with her various meltdowns, and, hey, karma's sweet. Certainly nothing to be ashamed of.

But *giggles?* That she hadn't had since she was an almost-was just thrilled to be close to the industry. With this guy, for whatever reason, she felt sixteen again, and ready to break sexual records and every flat surface in his house with fucking energetic enough to prove it. That seemed vaguely wrong to her, but whenever it occurred to her to worry about it a fresh wave of horniness rose up and drowned to impulse.

Pierce drove wild, but not *too* wild, his focus if anything improved by the distraction of her hand massaging his inner thigh, and the hot night air on Mulholland blew over them as he sped down one mountain road and up another, never hitting any red lights even when there were any lights to be seen, hugging the curves as the car were a matchbox toy riding on a grooved track. She would not have been surprised to see a loop-de-loop. She was halfway to the point of declaring "To hell with your house, just pull over the damn car," when he took a hard spin-out right into a switchback she hadn't spotted, performed a couple of additional zigzags, then *launched* the car up a slope so vertical she wouldn't have been surprised had it been intended as a take-off ramp to clear the next canyon entirely, and zipped into the U-shaped driveway of a mountaintop home so artfully hidden by landscaping that she wouldn't have suspected it of being there even if equipped with a map, a GPS program, and a helicopter.

The manse before them was like a glass modern monstrosity, all right angles and transparencies, as dark as the *2001* monolith complete with the stars that could be seen through it -- stars, she noted, far more numerous through the glass than they were in the surrounding sky.

"You've got to be kidding me! This is where you *live?*"

He twirled his keys. "Company house. Mine's on the beach. I don't think either one of us wanted to drive that far."

His delivery was douchey as hell, and any other night would have changed her mind. But she didn't want to, not now, not when the most urgent thought on her mind was getting *inside*. She fell against him, still giddy, knowing this was stupid and reckless and crazy but for the moment not caring, almost hopping as they went up the three Spanish-tiled stairs to the front door, where he fumbled with the keys and they almost ended up not waiting to get inside.

Then she performed a personal inventory of competing urges and said, "Come on, come on, I've got to go," and he managed to get the key working, and they went inside to what turned out to be a jungle.

All her life she had never been able to keep a plant alive. She came from a family with a backyard garden and a Mom who had never been able to think of anything more enjoyable to occupy her weekend than stabbing her patch of backyard dirt with a spade, but none of this had followed her down the birth canal. She had always been appalled when given potted plants as house-warming presents, because it had never been more than a matter of time before her unerring reverse skill with the plant kingdom turned even the hardiest perennial into a resentful corpse. As a failure at the art she tended to scowl hate at homes that functioned as warehouses for ferns, but she had never before seen any place so ruled by the verdant thumb that it aspired to the rain forest. There was a tree at the center of it, a great big green labyrinth of sprawling branches reaching up toward a ceiling that too shrouded by jungle canopy for a clear view. Around it, ferns, rubber plants, hanging vines, the unmistakable scent of rich soil and the nearby sound of a brook, babbling over polished stones. An array of tiny spot bulbs imbedded in whatever the place had for a ceiling stood in for distant stars. There was even a moon, providing enough light for navigation, and making the actual turning-on of the house lights redundant.

Her sense of wrongness nagged at her again. "What the hell --"

"It's the project house," he said, not elaborating, getting that out of their way before taking her by the hand and leading her through a gap in the undergrowth down a hallway carpeted in something that looked like -- no, dammit, didn't "look like," actually *was* -- grass. A recognizable doorway to her left was ajar enough to reveal more greenery but thank God a shower and a toilet to provide proof she hadn't somehow passed beyond the boundaries of civilization. This placated her until he led her to the master bedroom, where the illusion went into overdrive. He raised the dimmer switch to a low twilight and revealed walls covered with a permanent frieze of palm fronds, which swayed to and fro in response to ambient winds. Ambient noise reflected the buzzing of insects and the chattering of monkeys. An irregular jagged shape that could only be a bed but looked more like a rock ledge protruded from a wall that looked like a granite cliff side and featured waterfalls trickling through channels in the rock. And, holy crap, she hadn't been imagining things. She actually did hear jungle drums, somewhere not far away.

The waterfall in particular was a garish arrangement that struck her as certain to cause constant sleep-destroying piss urges throughout the night for anybody who might have wanted to sleep in this room, but right now it struck her with an absolute lack of aesthetic irony as the hottest stage for sex she had ever seen. She was the girl who even at a wide-eyed and coked-up twenty-two hadn't been able to keep a straight face for ten minutes when her guy of the time had treated her to an allegedly kinky weekend in the Caveman Room of the Madonna Inn -- though that was at least partially his fault; no adventurous lovers should ever attempt role-playing of any kind if they don't have the slightest skill at acting. But this was so far beyond artifice and cheese that it burned her.

She thought, *all this place needs is a tiger*, and couldn't put away the impression that she felt one, lurking just out of sight.

She tore off her glittery white top. "Seriously?"

"Seriously."

"But what the hell --"

"Project house," he said again, and this was the only explanation he had time for beforehand, because honestly she couldn't take it anymore.

What followed passed in a fever. She rode him, her eyes closed, her passion increasing with every moment, her conscious mind surrendering to the primitive hardwired part of her that didn't need to exist in any moment but this one. Thoughts like *the best ever* flitted through her head, only to become a drumbeat by themselves as she came faster and easier than she ever had, only to enter the build to another one. It wasn't love-making. It wasn't even sex, or the category of sex known as *screwing* that she'd always enjoyed the most no matter what degree of personal attachment she'd happened to feel for any particular partner. It was frenzy, every animal part of her wholly at home in a false jungle she'd allowed herself to believe in completely, as she and Pierce went at it with the fervent heat of creatures evolved to do nothing else.

Reality, of a sort, returned after she slid off him and stared blinking at the ceiling, wondering what the hell had just happened. Everything trying to be rational in her assured her that it hadn't been all that great. Pierce was avid, but on a technical level no better than competent, perhaps even a little on the selfish side. Sunny herself had been driven, but so overwhelmed by the intensity of her surroundings that she'd forgotten almost all her technique and devolved to her teenage self in terms of skill. But none of that had mattered. In this house, in this bed, with that wildness surrounding her and those distant jungle drums reverberating in her blood, the result was so clearly transcendent that decompressing was like coming back from the moon.

"Pierce, what the hell *is* this?"

"Pretty awesome, if you ask me."

"I thought so too, but, again, what the hell *is* it?"

"What do you *think* it is?"

Somewhere past the illusory surrounding trees, monkeys chattered in panic as something spooked them into fleeing in all directions. She didn't see any of them, but she heard rustling in any number of likely spots to her left, to her right…to where she lay, her skin slick with sweat that drifted off her skin as vapor, even as she watched. "I mean this funhouse. Is this some kind of company fuck pad or what?"

He laughed. "I won't say we haven't just used it that way, or that we're even the first. But no."

"You called it a…project house?"

"Yeah. Want a drink?"

One of the irregular boulders on the side of the irregular bed proved to have a lid, which opened to reveal a mini-bar. She rested her cheek on her hand, watching He sat in a way that allowed her to see him in profile, displaying the look she'd always hated seeing in some men after sex, the look of a cat proud to have tracked and devoured a canary. It was the kind of look that implied she'd been tricked and not wooed. It frankly made her hate him, a little, which bothered her because it underlined that part of her had been trying and failing to hate him all along.

"You, my dear, have just been introduced to my baby TIM."

"If that's the name for a body part, I'm leaving."

"Funny. Naaah, it's an acronym. Total Immersion Media. It's the reason Whizzards is about to make everybody who got in on the ground floor one of the top point one percent. Not top one percent. Top point one percent. I own eight points and I'm still gonna be richer than God. And that's just the current generation, 1.0. You just got a taste of some of the features of 2.0."

The speech sounded rote, like something he recited on a daily basis. It was another reason to hate him, though that too went away immediately.

Regarding TIM, she remembered being briefed in full, some familiar voice in an intimate setting telling her all about this cool new technology Whizzards was about to come out with. But she couldn't place the name or summon any of the specifics. Much more immediate was a shape she thought she saw prowling through the underbrush, a long and powerful shape, golden-brown with camouflaged with stripes that, in a heartbeat, rendered it once again invisible. Of course. *Wish for it, and it will come.*

"Can I have that drink now?"

He handed her a shot, poured one for himself, then knee-walked back to her side and drew close. "I'm about ready for another go."

So was she, almost; she felt the heat rising even now, and though it was welcome found herself distrusting it, almost fearing it, as she'd always needed a greater interim than this. She downed the shot and said, "Those plants were real. This bed is real. Even that grass in the hallway is real."

"Well, of course. They're all set up to help keep you in the proper state of mind, like those temple ruins you walk through before you get on an Indiana Jones simulator ride at a theme park. TIM's always more effective the more corroborative sensory reinforcement you start with."

She wasn't sure she got it and certainly didn't know whether she would get it even if he went through all the specs of what it was and how it worked, but even with her heart beginning to race again and the need rising in her like a fire, she flashed back to her Prius, still valet-parked at the party.

That lead to an associated thought of just why she'd been at the party in the first place, a question that seemed terribly important but also terribly remote, until a familiar face emerged out of the fog and was followed a fraction of a second later by a name

Josh

six years her junior and a software genius of some kind he assured her he also considered boring to talk about, actual *fan* of hers if you could believe such an insane thing, awkward and geeky and sweet in the precise combination that could render such ingredients hot

Josh

who had been hurt by life in some way and had come out of with this helpless little hiccup of a stammer, not a bad one, but the kind Hugh Grant had driven to fame and fortune; one he apologized for but that she loved

Josh

who who'd done some subcontracting work for Whizzards and had been the one to tell her what they were up to; some kind of signal that boosted the hindbrain and made media input so visceral that the most exquisitely rendered 3-D looked like childish scribbles on construction paper.

Josh, who had said something about it suppressing the brain's bullshit filters and maximizing the illusion.

Josh, who delighted her by being a man without having giving up being a boy, both in bed and out, and who she had already decided she would say yes to, the *big* yes to, whenever he got around to asking the question that was clearly burning inside him. Josh, who had sure as hell been working up to *something* when the TIME cover boy interrupted the conversation to say, "Hey, Joshie, can I borrow you a bit?" and lead him off into the noisy mob of the buzzed or about to be, leaving Sunny alone on the couch for Pierce to find.

She had somehow completely forgotten Josh, up until this moment, and now that she remembered him she was heartbroken and mortified, holding on to that sweet face even as the molten desire for Pierce rose up and threatened to drown it.

The music had been loud and the party had been fueled by booze and any number of white powders being passed around freely, but that much she was accustomed to seeing, whether she blessed it with her active participation or not.

Still, now that she had a brief moment of clarity, hadn't there been more going on there than even she had ever encountered, in this town? Had she actually when drinking and snorting, when come to think of it she'd left both things behind with the silly-twat era, had indeed been almost evangelical about her sobriety for some years now? Or had her head only been feeling that way? Had that Oscar-winning director on the balcony been enjoying a friendly avuncular chat with that up and coming Disney Channel tween, as Sunny's mind preferred to remember, or had she been flat on her back, her adolescent legs wrapped around his fat ass as he pumped her with his pants bunched up around his ankles? Had that long line at the buffet table been for the food or the noted talk show hostess who'd stripped and draped herself across the table, eager to take any man who lined up with his equipment at the proper altitude? If the *Time* magazine cover boy had really led Josh away to discuss business, how come they'd been holding hands and heading upstairs? Surely not all of that was true! But how much? Was it all or nothing? Was this all fantasy being built up in her mind now, or was it all memory, sights and sounds she had not been permitted to register while it was happening?

You son of a bitch! You and your fucking sociopath company used this TIM shit to roofie everybody!

Pierce was in a awkward, off-balance position. He was supported by one hand and one leg as he rolled toward her, empty space visible between the bed and his bare chest. He was in the middle of rolling toward her, to take the top position this time, and in less than a second he'd be on her, which she found she wanted more than anything she'd ever wanted in her whole life, more than fame and more than fortune and more than love and even more than she wanted to kill this son of a bitch while she still had a chance. It was only because she was also an animal feeling the presence of that hungry tiger in the underbrush, stalking her, eager for its chance to rip and rend, that she was able to follow the survival instinct over the passion instinct and do what needed to be done. She pressed the palms of both hands against Pierce's bare chest and shoved him away, with a strength that she had never been able to summon in everyday life, a strength representing what would surely be the last fight she had in her before whatever TIM was doing to her finished jacking her hindbrain for another go.

And maybe it was only because she'd been rendered half-feral from this TIM voodoo working its magic within her and maybe it was because Pierce happened to be balanced on two points and maybe because her finally emergent hatred for him had its required effect, but the shove had its desired effect. He didn't just fall back, he *rolled* back, his free arm flailing, and his mouth agape in surprise. She recorded the moment as a mental snapshot and had no trouble registering that even now he was no more than amused. He thought their play had only gotten a little rougher and fully expected her to jump after him and land on top. Then he went over the edge and instead of just rolling over onto the floor with a thud, slammed the back of his head against the rock sculpture.

Take a handful of pencils, between five and ten of them, wrap them in a bundle and get some steroid junkie to break that bundle in half. You'll have the sound Pierce made when he hit.

Sunny rolled after him, intent on screaming various epithets about rapists with small dicks, but even she peered over the side of the bed she knew that immediate future included achieving room temperature. The mingled horror and satisfaction she felt at the sight was boosted by the uninvited magic of TIM, calling forth another orgasm so powerful she cried out and came treacherously close to begging the unseen system for more. The tiger she couldn't stop herself from sensing in the undergrowth chuffed, matching her arousal with his hunger. But when it ebbed Pierce still lay motionless, his naked body horizontal against the floor while his head remained a ninety-degree vertical against the rocks. He had the stupidest and most gobsmacked look on his face that Sunny had ever seen on any man: and that included the universally idiotic look that their mugs all seemed to default to during orgasms. This was the face of a man who just didn't understand a goddamned thing about how it had come to this, and the main reason she wished he wasn't dead or real close to it was that she would have liked to spend some more time explaining it to him.

Sunny wasn't sorry, not exactly -- she was too filled with rage and shackled to the rhythm of those distant jungle drums to be sorry -- but neither was she immune to the jolt of panic that comes with *oh god no what have I done* and the question of how she was going to get anybody to understand that it had been an accident committed in the act of self-defense and that she'd been operating under diminished capacity anyway. *You son of a bitch look what you made me do* and she was not sorry for him so much as herself because even if the extenuating circumstances kept her out of trouble this would always be a part of her life now *SHIT I'm screwed* because if this went public she would always be the girl who threw a bastard out of bed so hard she freaking killed him.

Two things kept her from total paralysis.

The first was that five years as a working actress -- five years that had known their share of molestation, from the wandering hands of asshole stars to the smarmy suggestions of those who had wanted her to believe in the curative potential of sex demanded in exchange for *quid pro quo*. She had never said yes and never known what that dirtbag Todd Akin had called legitimate rape, either forcible or enabled by the pharmaceutical equivalent of whatever TIM was. But she had sure as hell been vaccinated by regular exposures to those who woulda if they coulda, and was equipped to disregard the crawling ickiness long enough to act.

The other was

SHIT Josh

The maniacs still had him and they were doing God-Alone-Knew-What to him.

They *had* to be maniacs. It followed. Any run-of-the-mill evil piece of shit could do what the run-of-the-mill evil pieces of shit in this town did, when were not just evil pieces of shit but also happened to be rich and/or powerful; for folks of that altitude it wasn't too much of a stretch to beat up a girlfriend or slaughter an ex-wife or shoot a house guest in the face or rape a pre-teen girl in a hot tub and somehow believe that celebrity would save them, because it so often had. Famous predator, obscure victim: that may have been screwed-up math, but at least it was math you could understand an evil shit famous egomaniac believing.

But the Whizzards bunch had taken it to the next level. They'd cast their evil spell on a large part of the A-list, and they'd done it without once imagining that there could be consequences. That was not just garden-variety off-the-shelf crazy. That was leaving the planet. Maybe it was just the way they were and maybe exposure to their own product had deranged them. But there was no way of knowing what else they were prepared to do.

And they had Josh.

She speed-crawled back over the bed that was not a bed, looking for her clothes. All around her the jungle kept its counsel, birds screeching siren-like to alert others in their perches at the treetops; the monkeys howling, the mosquitoes droning. The hot moist air wafted over her, bringing with it the rich scents of soil and dead things being swarmed by ants. A deeper smell, rich, powerful, feline, *tiger*, drifted by as dense as a wave breaking on some Indian ocean shore, and even as she found her bra she also found the unwanted images rising out of her most secret places: an image of herself lying warm and submissive against hard stone while a king of beasts buried its snout in her. She gasped and wept and found her panties and her glittery white top and tried to keep hold of the sane and rational and civilized parts of herself long enough to remember how to get dressed.

No amount of rational thought was enough to dispel the layers of illusion that were if anything growing ever more vivid around her, the illusion that she was not in some mountaintop near LA but instead in some primordial place, *the* primordial place, being stalked by forces that hungered to consume her.

Maybe she shouldn't have dressed at all. Maybe she should have run out the front door as she was. Maybe the best thing she could have done was flee naked into the night, trusting that she wouldn't run into any more predators of either the two-legged or four-legged variety. But clothing, thin and inadequate as it was, was armor. Clothing was civilization. Clothing was a reminder of who she was. She pulled on her pants and almost doubled over from the sudden wave of raw need that rose up from the parts of her TIM was awakening, but fought the wave back and stumbled away from the ledge-shaped platform bed, foregoing any attempt to find her shoes.

She had the idea she would lose herself if she wasted the time it would take to try to find her shoes.

The floor beneath Sunny's bare feet now felt like it was ankle-deep in snakes, long black venomous things that hissed as she picked her way among them. Gnats flew at her eyes, each one drawing close with an angry whine before veering off, for another dive-bombing charge at her boiling blood. She slapped at one on her arm and was not surprised to see the red spot left behind. One of the snakes reared back and sank fangs into her ankle, the pain even more sharp and real for being imaginary. She wondered if TIM was powerful enough to make imaginary venom pulse through her veins, swelling her tissues, making her flesh black and necrotic. By now she would not be surprised. Another snake struck. She snarled and ground its noxious little head under her heel, grinding it into the imaginary dirt, hearing it hiss as its skull collapsed and it died.

This, too, aroused something primitive inside her. The urge to rip off her clothes, flee back to the bed and masturbate herself into a coma was overwhelming but deadly; instead she took a fold of cheek between her teeth and bit down, hard, tears welling from her eyes as her mouth filled with the taste of blood.

The tiger, still not visible but so close that her chest ached from the force of her fear of it, roared.

Sunny rounded the edge of the platform bed and reached the cairn of stones where that smug predatory lying piece of shit goddamned asshole fuckstain Pierce had left his carefully folded pants. His wallet, bulging with platinum cards, lay on top like an offering to the Gods as did his car keys and his cell phone. She squeezed the keychain before she put it away as well, willfully driving the sculpted shaft into her palm, seeking focus in the pain.

A single thought, wisdom she'd learned from any number of mystery novels and *Law & Order* marathons, bubbled up through the fog: *You don't want to flee the scene. You don't want to leave without at least trying to call him an ambulance or something. That's admitting guilt. That's the kind of thing Sam Waterston lectures the jury about, just before the defendant of the week gets life.*

She glanced at Pierce. He lay covered in a carpet of red ants. It was at least an inch thick, so dense that his shape could now only be perceived by the shape of the feeding frenzy, his outline rendered Michelin-Man vague by the sheer number of hungry mandibles involved; layers and layers of them, the ones on top burrowing deeper into the mass of their brethren to get to the flesh of the meat that had fallen. She remembered mythologies of army ants who periodically sprung up out of jungle to march in their billions across the landscape, devouring every living thing they encountered down to the bones. The Pierce-shape seem to be flattening, even as she watched. It wasn't much of a stretch to picture the swarm's group-mind registering that the last morsel had been picked clean of the last bleached bone and moving on in search of other sustenance.

Fuck it, I'll use his phone to call from the car.

She took the phone and turned toward the hallway, stumbling over snakes, brushing fern leaves aside as the corridor ahead became a narrow dirt path, that had at some point in the distant past been carved out of impenetrable wilderness by sweaty men with machetes. Just before she passed out the bedroom hallway a furious snarl erupted to her immediate right, and she whirled and took a single furious step back, catching a glimpse of two golden-green eyes, filled with terrible knowledge, peering at her from a gap in the undergrowth. A leg tipped with claws like sickles, claws capable of penetrating all the way to the bone and rendering her a catch that could be drawn in and eviscerated, shot out and sliced the air where she had been.

She was wise enough to know that this had not been a serious attempt to catch her. That had been an exploratory poke, the kind of thing house cats do when they chase the red dots projected by laser pointers.

Worse was coming.

She spun and fell into the hallway, propped up by the wall, a wall that comforted her by feeling like a wall but which to her TIM-addled senses also insisted on rustling like the fronds of underbrush too thick to pass. She launched herself away from that wall and rebounded off the other, moving forward in a zigzag pattern as if that was the only way she could, as if she'd become a sailboat fighting weather that forced her to tack against the wind. Distant baboon shrieks mocked her as her face smacked into the first of the real plants and she ripped it away with a vicious snarl.

Behind her something huge and animal and hungry made a thump as it hit the bedroom floor. The padding sound of its footsteps grew louder and closer together behind her.

She ran.

How long could the hallway be? Fifteen, twenty feet at most? It elongated now, becoming an endless route through patches of green and shadow, over ground that was not just the grass she remembered but also a litter of sticks and pebbles and fallen leaves, interrupted here and there by narrow streams. Behind her the footsteps of the tiger, which in a world of normal physics would have caught up with her in a leap or two, remained just a step or two behind, so close that she could feel the hot moist huffs of its breath through the material of her top. It yowled in rage and warning and she could hardly breathe out of terror and her ankle caught in a gnarled root protruding from the soil and she went down face-first in mud.

The tiger landed on her.

It hit with the weight and force of any real full-grown tiger, between seven and eight hundred pounds of it. Her ribs avoided cracking only because the soil beneath her was soft and the weight on her back only drove her deeper into the filth and ooze of the earth. Eight points of pain erupted like flame where its claws stapled her shoulder blades. Another piercing snarl burst from a mouth now just behind her vulnerable neck, a mouth that was less than a heartbeat away from ripping out her spine and tasting the sweet copper tang of her blood. The claws snagged on the false skin of her top and drew back, tearing deep gouges in the fabric and etching what had to be ugly scars in the skin of her back: more idle exploration by a predator who had more than enough time to play.

Except that this was bullshit and there was no tiger and she would *not die in this candy-ass stupid way.*

She once again bit her cheek hard enough to taste blood and thought *Josh* and *bastards* and *there's no goddamned tiger* and sunk her fingers into the mud *there's no goddamned mud* and pulled herself forward out of the muck *there's no goddamned muck* and took a breath of fresh air and got her knees under her and stood, the weight on her back lessening with each moment from the back breaking burden it had been seconds before to a weight closer to a house cat's. The monkeys continued to shriek *there are no goddamned monkeys* and the underbrush continued to block the way in front of her *it's just a goddamned corridor* and *it's all just special effects* and it's *no more than some signal overriding your bullshit filters* and *you can block it out.*

The nonexistent claws raked her back again, a fiery burst of agony that threatened to drive away what sanity she still had. Her shirt was peeled away, just the first and most harmless layer in a striptease that would in another moment include her skin, her flesh, her muscles and her organs. *It's not real* but the tiger off her long enough to bat her in play and she rolled, looking up at the face of the beast itself, with the bloody and shredded remains of her top dangling from its mouth. She could see the stars in the ceiling through it, but the shirt and the blood were clearly real, and the beast itself was somehow physical enough to wreak the damage the illusion demanded.

She drove her elbows into the grass and back-crawled, giving the tiger a kick in the face for good measure. It recoiled, not hurt, but startled. It actually backed up a step, considering what to do. Maybe a real tiger would have been better at killing her and maybe it would have also retreated from a kick, but either way that didn't matter. It was enough for this thing not quite a tiger that she was dealing with. She staggered to her feet, unsurprised as one of the shreds of her top sloughed away from her as she did and just as unsurprised to see strip of cloth tinged with scarlet.

Just before she turned her back on the big cat she saw it tensing its hind legs for another leap and knew that if it brought her down again there was no way it would let her get up a second time.

She cut a hard left at the end of the hallway, a rabbit who was not as fast as the predator on her tail but better than it ever could be at changing direction quickly. The hot breeze of its passage stung the stripes on her back a fraction of a second before it landed at the base of the hall's giant, ceiling-scraper of a tree. She grabbed two of the potted palms as she passed them, pulling them over onto the ground to make an obstacle course of the floor between the tiger and the front door; she knew it not be enough, not for a creature with the strength of a battering ram who could leap twenty feet, but as a snarl ripped the air behind her she toppled a second palm and then a third.

As she reached the front door and impossibly succeeded in opening it the crack she needed to escape she looked over her shoulder and saw that the outcome of the next half second or two would be too close to call. The tiger was only a few feet away, racing toward her with lowered head, its green-yellow eyes a pair of cold jewels ablaze in the night. They were lasers, those eyes, fixed on Sunny as the sole focus of its killing hunger. It seemed to be in no particular hurry, the palms toppled on the living room tile no hindrance at all as it simply padded over the obstacles without looking at them. She could no longer see through it. It seemed bigger than any tiger she had ever seen at any zoo, and as it drew close it seemed to be changing shape to form a more primal fantasy, its stripes fading and its canine teeth elongating to primordial sabers.

Sunny slipped through the tiny crack of the doorway and was just starting to pull the door after her when a massive weight struck the other side hard enough to shut the door and send her flying backward. She tripped as she backed off the first of the three steps leading down to the driveway, and fell backward, landing butt-first on the blacktop. Her head whipped back and hit the earth a second later, with an impact that hurt enough to dizzy her but seemed to bring make the world shake and clarify, like a TV image improved by a hard slap to the receiver.

Sunny expected to die a second later, but the tiger was nowhere to be seen.

Any hopes that it had gone away were dispelled by the dreadful pounding from the project house's front door. It was the huge, ravenous and pissed-off sound common to things in cages that know satisfying meals to be just beyond their reach. She didn't have to see what the tiger was doing to know that it was ramming the door again and again, in the furious belief it would be able to break through. Sunny couldn't say it was wrong. It wasn't real, not in any sense she understood, but it had possessed enough of a physical presence to rip her shirt and her back to shreds, not to mention slam that door; it seemed more impossible some-how now that she was free of the house and at least a little removed from what the technological wizardry inside had done to her, but somehow, TIM had summoned it, turned it from a thing that had only been felt to a thing that existed, a thing with weight, that could kill. Hell, the same could probably be said of the ants she'd seen swarming Pierce.

Where had all that come from? She couldn't imagine the resourceful corporate sociopaths at Whizzards actually stocking their test house with army ants and a shape-shifting sabertooth. They had both come out of the illusion. They had become real, physically real, out of the illusion. Out of *her* illusion.

This made no sense to her, and that at last was the straw too heavy for her to take. She couldn't afford to stay here. It wasn't safe, and there was still Josh to save. But she was also human, and with the immediate threat evaded she lost a few seconds to registering the pain and the fear and the mixed feelings of betrayal and violation and self-pity, as well as the sheer disorienting weight of the world itself changing rules on her. Tears welled, the stars above her blurred, and she whispered, "You sons of bitches," meaning not just Pierce and not the entire gang of sociopaths at Whizzards but everybody who had put together the infrastructure of the whole damn world, that there should be this kind of thing in it.

It couldn't have been more than a couple of seconds.

Then she heard wood splinter.

The front door, solid as it had to be, now had a jagged white crack running from the top of the frame to the bottom.

That crack bulged and dislodged white splinters as something of impossible power struck it again.

She thought *that's impossible! Even a tiger can't do that!* followed by *it's an imaginary tiger, it can do whatever it wants!* followed by MOVE, MOVE, MOVE, which got her to her feet and lurching in a broken Caliban gait to the parked Ferrari.. The pounding against the door to the house was still continuing when she slid behind the wheel, her injured back screaming at its first contact with the leather of the bucket seat.

She took a deep breath, for the first time registering the difference between the air outside and the air she'd breathed inside. What surrounded her was no longer the thick humid musk of a generic rain forest, but the hot dry air Angelenos know, the kind that can suck all the moisture from the back of your throat in a handful of breaths. Her throat, already dry from panic that followed, went parched. She was still rational enough to remember her moral and legal requirement to call help for Pierce, even if he was beyond profit from it. She took his cell from her pocket and dialed 911, letting it ring twice before she tossed it out the window and into the rock garden. Now they couldn't say she hadn't called.

Then she used Pierce's key to start his car.

She felt the magnitude of her error the second the engine revved.

The unwanted burning heat radiated from her loins, spreading up her spine and down her arms and legs, making her want Pierce more than she'd ever wanted any other man who'd ever lived, while the air itself turned moist with rain-forest humidity and the night turned dense with the beating of jungle drums.

Shit

That's why it didn't wear off when we left the party

Sunny gasped and whimpered no and for the life of her, literally, could not remember how to drive a car. All around her, the mountain-top seemed to shimmer, first with heat and then with transformation, the darkness becoming speckled, the space between her and the house becoming striped with the trees that had chosen just that moment to announce their presence.

A hole tore open in the door to the project house. A bloody muzzle with saber teeth poked through, the teeth closing on the splintered hole and gnawing the edges to enlarge the one route to their prey. Sunny wanted to scream at the creature, ordering it to go back, suggesting it make its meal out of the human being still in the house who was dead and therefore an easy meal…but of course the ants had taken Pierce. The tiger was well within its rights to demand a less sullied meal.

And there was also this: against her will, Sunny was turned on. The thought of being ravaged by that tiger burned in her as if it was something she could possibly want, something she had always wanted to take pleasure in. The thought made her shudder with something other than fear and made her squirm where she sat, delaying the action necessary to save her life until the tiger had the feline brainstorm of attacking the doorjamb and the ruined remains of the door flew open, revealing the beast in all its terrible glory.

The house had not been able to contain it

The open Ferrari would not provide any protection at all.

For an instant the tiger stood framed in the doorway, somehow contained by it while remaining too big for it. It took up more space than the space it took up. It was titanic, unstoppable, not just a tiger but the ultimate tiger, and when it roared, its teeth growing longer and more like scimitars with every heartbeat, it sounded savage enough to eat the world.

Then it charged.

Sunny rammed the Ferrari into reverse and floored it. Even as she achieved speed the view through the windshield was no longer dominated by the house, but instead by the tiger, which was less than a car-length ahead of her and didn't have even an iota of difficulty keeping pace. She shrieked at it, dragging the primitive vocabulary of pure fear and hatred from her lungs as the car reversed and the tiger remained the exact same apparent size in the glass.

Pursued by the tiger, the Ferrari flew down the sloped end of the diveway, bumped violently rolling over a flagstone or something, scraped pavement at the spot where the driveway hit the road, and kept going. It crossed the street entirely, and bottomed out again as it hit the gully on the other side. Sunny remembered the switchback, braked too late and came to a stop with the Ferrari's ass hanging over a sheer slope leading down to the road's next lower level, maybe a hundred feet below. Managing to stop at all was sheer luck, but it left her with no time to put the car in drive and roar back to the road she'd just left, because that's when the tiger leaped and landed with its hind legs on the hood and its front legs on a windshield that spider-webbed with the impact.

The Ferrari shuddered at the edge and began to tip.

The tiger scrabbled for purchase on the glass, crumpling it further before managing to grab hold at the top and swipe at Sunny with its other paw, the slash passing so close to Sunny's eyes that for an instance her vision consisted of nothing but a streak of orange.

Then the glass crumpled the rest of the way and the tiger was on her: a nightmare of fur and musk and animalistic hunger and snarling rage.

At the same time the car finished tipping and started to roll. The slope down to the next switchback was not quite completely vertical, and the car, propelled in in large part by the panicked reflex that led her to floor the gas again, had no problem racing downhill toward what promised to be a catastrophic landing. It would have been a terrifying ride without the weight of a ravenous uber-tiger and the influence of TIM to jack it higher, but with both working their primitive magic on Sunny's head the landscape around her grew more frightening still. The slope became a nightmarish still-life of twisting carnivorous vines with heads like snapping great whites, grasping for car and tiger and woman as they all fell together. Sunny even felt the last of her civilized self give way, and experienced the tang of her own blood as the aftertaste of some kill she'd brought down herself, after a satisfying chase through the jungle's darkest places.

In the last instant before the Ferrari struck bottom she didn't scream. She roared, the sound far louder and more animalistic than she ever could have made with a pair of merely human lungs.

The Ferrari would not have been able to reverse down the hill indefinitely even if the gully between the slope and the next lower layer of switchback had not been there to catch it. Its front end, unbalanced by the weight of the tiger and losing traction in the dirt, had already begun to shimmy, tipping over toward the driver's side in a disastrous turn that in another hundred feet or so would have caused it to start somersaulting as it sped the rest of the way down. But the gully was there to catch it, and as the rear end crumpled from the bone shattering impact, the front end tipped over, and both the lady and the tiger -- neither secured by seat belt -- hurtled backward, free of the car.

Of course, with TIM still working in her head, Sunny did not experience the next second as deadly free fall and the precursor to a personal splatter. She experienced it as flight. She was a goddess, mistress of the wilderness below her, and all the lights of the city in the distance were not avenues and boulevards but the signal fires of tribesmen who worshipped her. She had come to Hollywood all those years ago to become a goddess of sorts, and had failed; but in this moment she knew what was like, to float above it all serene and savage, to be aware that she could command any one of those lights and any one of the shivering primitives gathered for safety around it with a flick of her finger. In the instant before she landed, she felt her shoulder-length hair erupt from her scalp and become a glorious waist-length mane, spreading out in all directions like a fiery corona.

The Ferrari completed its flip and slammed into the road.

Sunny was about to land in a feline crouch with no injury at all when TIM blinked out. The drumbeat ended and reality intruded. She became what she usually was, saw the pavement race up at her, and for a fraction of a second surrendered to common sense and her rational understanding of what was possible and what was not. She still landed on her bare feet, but not with the graceful roll that might have been in her a second before. Instead what arrived was the most powerful impact she had ever felt. Her legs buckled instead of breaking and she rolled twice, each secondary impact a fresh manifestation of pain, scraping her feet, knees and elbow bloody. She rolled twice, felt all breath knocked from her lungs, and landed face down. She coughed, pushed against the road surface with both arms, felt a jab of pain, and collapsed, all fight gone.

She had failed herself and she had failed Josh and she was just a battered thing, listening for the sound of sirens. Weeping, she damned this town, damned the monsters at Whizzards who had done this to her, damned every mistake she had ever made.

She heard a car coming, and looked down the slope, where a cop car was making its way up the switchback. It was only two or three rises below, and would be up to where she knelt in a couple of minutes. Maybe it would be enough to wait for their arrival of the police and dump all of this in their laps.

But that was before she heard something that would reach her first.

The tiger.

She lifted her head and saw it, padding slowly toward her. It was larger than ever, but it had not been at all enhanced by this latest spurt of growth; closer now to elephant scale, it had not retained all of its prior physicality, but instead dissipated, becoming once again something that could be seen through, something that was wispier and dreamier and less solid with every limping step. Its roar, when it came, was a weak cough, no more than an interruption in the still night air. Nothing about it suggested magnificence, let alone hunger. It was no threat to her. Maybe if it fled back up the hill and returned to the vicinity of the project house, within the zone which TIM still affected, it would have been returned to its old self; but with the house out of range and the TIM connection in the car shattered by the impact, there was nothing in range capable of maintaining it.

It was dying.

Sunny staggered to her feet, moaned as her right leg rebelled at the prospect of supporting her weight, and braced herself for an attack. She had to; there was no possibility of running.

But no attack came. The tiger made its way across a minefield of stones and broken glass, lowered its fading head, and head-butted her, its throat vibrated with this, its final salute. Against all odds, a lump grew in her own throat as she clutched the great head at both sides, and rested her own against its forehead.

She considered everything yet to come: the arrival of the police, the inevitable questions, the Whizzards scum buying their way out of trouble as their kind always did; her relationship with Josh hanging on a little longer but almost certainly failing as everything that had happened in the last couple of hours refused to vacate the fraught space between them.

And if she became a part of the story? Her name being used as the punchline of filthy dismissive jokes on late night TV. And the internet;

oh, God, the internet. The photoshopped memes. The endless savaging of her name in chat rooms. All that crap she'd evaded, by leaving the world of acting, would now rise up like a tsunami of toxic waste and engulf her, in a world where she'd also have to watch the geniuses behind TIM work out the bugs and grow richer than God transforming the media landscape to their own specifications.

The tiger was almost invisible now, and no heavier than a whiff of smoke. Sunny wasn't feeling much more substantial herself. The cop car was still working its way up the hill. She had a heartbeat, maybe less, before it was too late.

But that heartbeat would be more than long enough, because she knew what she had to do.

In the end, the point was this.

In one past life, Sunny had been an actress. In retrospect, she had to admit that she hadn't been a very good one. Even if she'd had the right luck and gotten the right role and claimed the prominence she'd wanted, she never would have been one of the immortals who held on for a lifetime. She would have faded back to obscurity within a very few years, almost certainly by now.

But she'd known the trick. She'd lived the life. She'd dealt with the crap that went with it and eaten more than her share of it in her brief quest to become one of the names.

However good she was, illusion was no stranger to her, and neither was delusion.

Now that TIM had shown her it could be done, she didn't need any brilliant technological developments to suppress her bullshit filters.

She placed a hand on each side of the tiger's head and put everything she had into not just suppressing them, but eradicating them.

The drumbeat began as wishful thinking, the kind of thing that could have been real and could have been just what she wanted to hear, but she *made* herself believe in it, *made* the air grow thick and humid and rich with the now welcome jungle corruption of the environment she sought. Believing in it even a little bit made it easier to summon more. The beat grew louder. The night turned sultry. The heat rose from inside her, making the air ripple, healing the tiger, making her own flesh knit, changing the very geography around her. The wrecked Ferrari combusted. The flames were too far away to burn to burn her, but they made the air hot, and she used that too, adding the fire's fury and heat and power to her own. She abandoned doubt. She made herself as much a creature of primitive hungers as the great cat growing more solid and vivid before her. She grew almost six inches. She felt herself changing, becoming taller, sleeker, more feline, more dangerous: all the things she needed to be, right now, in order to return to the Whizzards party and do what needed to be done.

By the time she was finished, the drumbeat was almost deafening. She didn't mind that, not really. It would be good, tonight, for that sound to follow her. Tonight, that sound could follow her as much as it wanted.

A pair of headlights appeared down the hill and for a moment caught her in a circle of harsh light.

In a rich and terrible new voice, she told the tiger, "Let's go."

It obediently fell into place at her side, and the two of them left the road to take the hills on foot, already anticipating a successful hunt.

THE MONKEY TRAP

Amber needed a book. It was *The Estates of Sarah Holliday*, a delicate comedy of manners following a young woman's trials and tribulations in 1870s New England, and it was the most obscure novel by one Charlotte Winsborough, a fussy and now almost completely forgotten nineteenth-century author Amber had chosen for her dissertation. Winsborough had enjoyed three decades of critical and commercial success in her own time, and was by about 1900 lionized as a female Twain. In modern times she was only remembered at all because one of her novels had been hauled from what was already obscurity to become an uncharacteristically sub-par Katherine Hepburn movie in 1943. Only a couple of the author's twenty-three novels remained in print now, but most could be tracked down through antiquarian booksellers or online sources, the one exception being *Estates*, which had achieved mild notoriety for its uncharacteristic sexual content and which was not to be found anywhere, not even at the university where her papers had been archived. Amber was about to surrender to the general belief among prior scholars that it was lost when a sympathetic professor gave her the address of a private dealer who had long been her own source for rarities.

"You will have to go to his home," the professor said. "The man does not have a telephone or a computer, and will only search his collection for you if you make an appointment. But I promise you, if the book exists anywhere on the planet, it's on his shelves."

Correspondence ensued, an appointment got made, and two weeks later, Amber carved out enough time for a road trip and a visit to a rambling old Victorian mansion of many turrets, existing on multiple acres in a space that had resisted the industrial small town that had grown up around it. The grounds were enclosed by a wrought-iron fence, the vast lawn was littered with the orange detritus of autumn, but pleasingly so, and the structure itself, which appeared in fine repair, screamed old money: just the right background for a man who had dedicated his life to an avocation as financially suspect as the accumulation and preservation of old books. On knocking, Amber was greeted by the man himself, who offered a slight bow, welcomed her to his home, and after a few questions about the volume she wanted, left her, in order to conduct his search. In the meantime, he invited Amber to browse the shelves on the ground floor, asking only that she refrain from entering any closed door or climbing the several staircases to upper levels.

Nothing had been organized in any manner Amber could immediately discern. Shelving was everywhere, bookcases literally on top of bookcases, and in places behind other bookcases, arranged on tracks so they could be shuffled for ease in searching. The collection started at the vestibule, continued in the foyer, and reached astonishing bounty in a cavernous chamber that showed signs of once being a ballroom but was now a literary warehouse. There were hallways narrowed to near impassibility by more shelving on each side, nooks and crannies that were stuffed with even more volumes, and second and third floor balconies lined with even more; possibly millions of volumes in all. Her eyes glazed at the sheer variety she could access even without trespassing into those areas she'd been forbidden to enter, a collection that included everything from garish science-fiction paperbacks to obscure eighteenth-century poetry to the memoirs of obscure Belgian politicians. Amber, who had before this moment considered herself the most voracious reader on the planet, who had been told as a child that she would ruin her eyes and that all her reading would rot her brain, could have spent her meager savings collecting a basket of volumes long on her personal wish list, were it not for the apparent total lack of organization that made finding any particular author an exercise in just wandering aimlessly and hoping for the best. She found mysteries stacked next to outdated automotive manuals, volumes of collected letters stacked next to sedate erotica of the 1920s, violent men's adventure novels stacked next to primers for first-graders. She saw books on top of books, books shelved four-deep, books tucked away in little alcoves that were features of the house's architecture, like a hollow she found on one wall that was clearly the negative space formed by the space between heating ducts, and that was stuffed solid with the yellowing religious tracts of a rather fussy Episcopal minister of the 1920s.

It all escaped total madness by visible organization within individual authors. Just by accident, Amber ran into shelves that included an exhaustive collection of works by the noir writer Cornell Woolrich, including editions written under his pseudonym William Irish. Rooms away, she found Ed McBain and Evan Hunter and Richard Marsten, the multiple pseudonyms of the writer born Salvatore Albert Lombino, also grouped in proximity. Elsewhere still she found Laura Ingalls Wilder and Harlan Ellison and Naguib Mahfouz, and in every single place where an author was shelved, a nearly-complete collection of that author's works all appeared in the same place, unmixed by that horror endemic to so many libraries and bookstores: the randomization caused when browsers pick up a volume, walk around for a while, and upon ultimately deciding against it, put it down in some completely inappropriate place. But there was no other visible organization, not by genre, not by alphabet, not by title, not by year of publication, and not even by format. The oversized books and the large print books were shoved in alongside the little paperbacks, the valuable books alongside the nearly-disposable detective pulps, and all of it at a density that threatened to make her eyes cross.

Amber had encountered disorganization on almost this level at used-book stores, including some where anything that came in was just dumped alongside anything that had already joined the collection, with the location of any desired volume left as an exercise for the shopper. To some degree, poring through such a teeming place could even be enjoyable, an activity to while away entire afternoons, with a basket full of discoveries at the end of them. But this was beyond surfeit, and the close grouping all the books within individual author name suggested some filing system beyond her, that she was failing to get. After a couple of hours, including some time lost in what amounted to a labyrinth, she finally found herself back in the parlor where the aged proprietor sat, perusing a thin book of poems in Japanese. *Estates* already sat in a prominent place before him.

The man was not old in the sense that Amber's father was old, which is to say a man in his early sixties who was robust but who had become a silver fox, weathered and respectable, secure in his place in the world. Nor was he old in the sense of Amber's grandfather, a man in his late eighties who, though his face had achieved the texture of old leather, regarded the world with eyes of astonishing blue, and still walked five miles a day, almost as energetically as he ever had, though now with a cane. The proprietor of the house was still spry, but old in the sense that Egyptian monuments are old, that crumbling old temples are old, that yellowing parchment is old. He wasn't decrepit. He looked like he'd outlived the layer of dust that he normally would have acquired by sheer antiquity, that he had cycled past his years as a fossil and become a permanent object, like a Swiss Alp. He wore antique spectacles, but the lenses did not possess the coke-bottle thickness that by magnifying the eyes give so very old people perpetually shocked expressions, and the architecture of the lower half of his face gave him a grin a little bit like a dolphin's, though there was a sardonic flavor to it, implying that while he'd seen it all, he hadn't approved of all of it. He asked if she'd enjoyed the tour through his home and seemed gratified when she confessed to being overwhelmed. He said that *The Estate of Sarah Holliday* had been exactly where he'd always known he would find it, on the third shelf of a utility closet on one of the upper floors.

He let her inspect the book. It was not a first edition, which she probably could not have afforded given its extreme rarity, but a little-known and (he said with a twinkle) highly unauthorized edition from 1895, published by a small Australian house that had produced a print run of four hundred copies without compensation to the author and promptly went out of business when their little act of piracy proved pointless in light of their nation's nigh-total lack of commercial interest. Almost all their copies had been destroyed when the warehouse holding the firm's assets burned, possibly by arson, and most of those that remained had suffered the usual fate that overcomes neglected and unloved books over years and decades. Still, a few had ended up in the hands of a tiny cabal of defiant Winsborough enthusiasts who had preserved them with the fanaticism only to be found among those who live through books. One volume had crossed oceans to wind up in his hands, on a shelf where it had been preserved by the insulating powers of the very books shelved on either side of it, and (in three layers), in front of it. Conditions had been perfect to defy entropy, and so here it was, a hardcover only slightly redolent of must, with pages that were yellow only at the edges, that were not at all brittle or loose, leaving a copy that could be read with genuine pleasure by a scholar who did not need to worry about it falling apart at her slightest touch: qualities that, he confessed, he could not say of every other Winsborough book in his collection. He named a price, which was just steep enough to make Amber wince without qualifying as an outright impossibility.

She wrote a check, he produced a receipt, and as he opened a drawer and removed a small brown bag to carry away her purchase, she could not help interjecting, "I have to ask. How can you find anything?"

He seemed to take deep pleasure in the question, which appeared to be a perennial. "I'm organized. I have an uncanny memory, and I know where every single book goes."

"I didn't see a system."

"That's good, young lady; that's deliberate. Some of my volumes are quite valuable. There are far too many for any burglar to cart off, most of them worthless except to enthusiasts of the writers involved, but any rival collectors who knew my system as well as I do would be able to break in on some day when I was not in residence and go straight to the shelf where I keep, for instance, my first edition Poe, my *Action Comics #1*, or my first folio Shakespeare. Better to avoid the dead giveaway of alphabetical order, or of subject matter, and keep everything stored according to a system that speaks to my own inclinations."

Amber could be cute when she wanted to be, sometimes very, and so she raised an arch eyebrow. "Oooh, mysterious."

"Not at all. I could tell you my system right now, and even if you were bent toward grand larceny the information would still be of no assistance to you, because it references a key that only I possess. The criterion I use for classification is simple enough. But only I have the access to the data it connects with, that places authors within those categories; only I know where they are shelved according to that criterion; and only I can tell you what subsidiary system I've used, to settle the many, many cases where an author qualifies for more than one category. So: what I am willing to tell you, right now, will not give anyone all the information required to rob me blind. But it will provide you with an academic point of interest." He had not yet placed the Winsborough in the paper bag, and so it was available for him to flourish, cover out, as illustration of his point. "Would you like to know?"

Amber saw something in the old man's expression that had not been there before: a craftiness, a ravenousness, a greed of the sort illustrated by the old silent-movie characterization of a villain, rubbing his hands with avarice as he beholds a hoard of gold coins. It was the same look she'd perceived in certain young men (and that older female professor) who had thought to lure her into a position where it would have been impossible to say *no*. It was the kind of look that left Amber mentally reviewing the route between her and the exit, the precise route to the spot where she'd parked her car, the speed she would have to run in order to escape, in case the old man turned out to be significantly faster than he looked.

And then she blinked, and it was like the fear that had just overcome her in the last heartbeat or so was all for nothing. Because he was just an old man, a collector who lived to acquire and sell rare books, who likely went days in silence conversing with no one but the authors moldering in the likely millions of pages stacked up in every corner of every hallway of this house; and even if he thought he had a dire secret, Amber did not imagine herself some fainting virgin incapable of bearing it.

"Sure."

"I categorize the authors by the worst sins they committed in life."

"Excuse me?"

"My practice is to obtain all the biographical information I can, something I happen to be very good at, and shelve everybody according to transgressions. The great twentieth century novelist Norman Mailer stabbed his wife while drunk; it's not the worst thing he ever did, but if it was, he would be in the place where I keep works by men who have assaulted women with knives. Another great twentieth-century author, William S. Burroughs, outright murdered his own wife by foolishly attempting to shoot a bottle off her head; alas, he was not up to the pictured feat of marksmanship, and so his works might well be shelved with the authors who took lives with stunts of extraordinarily stupid recklessness. It's not actually there, you understand; I happen to know something else he once did, something not known to the general public, that by my ratings system take precedence. My collection of the cartoonist Al Capp, creator of the beloved *L'il Abner*, is shelved along with other prolific serial rapists. John Lennon's written works are classified with the wife-beaters, Isaac Asimov's works with the serial sexual harassers. Theodore Sturgeon is, for a number of reasons, shelved among those who betray the trust of their friends. I classify the works of the science fiction writer known as James Tiptree Jr., pen name of Alice B. Sheldon, among the murder-suicides; the fantasist Marion Zimmer Bradley among those who abetted and were said to participate in horrific child abuse. I have rooms, entire rooms, dedicated to racists, to adulterers, to hypocrites, to collaborators who exploited and then ripped off their creative partners; to slanderers; to those who wrote of their own supposed heroism in war but inflated their own roles while denying credit to the dead who can no longer testify.

"There are large swaths of my collection dedicated to those who, as far as I can tell, abused only themselves: the drunks, the addicts, the ones who lived and died in paroxysms of self-involvement, bringing pain into the lives of their loved ones and immense irritation into the daily routines of associates who merely had to deal with them. Even the kind, the pleasant, the philanthropists, the ones remembered as saints: they were all guilty of something, however small, and I shelve them all in the places that strike me, according to my own personal criteria, as most characteristic, even if I have to seek out the indiscretions of youth, or the desperation that afflicts those in decline: such as one writer I know, a talented but commercially not a very successful one, who survived the cruelest poverty by hiding the death of her mother and continuing to cash the social security checks. I happen to possess such a constitutional affinity for such attributes that the name of any author whose works I've obtained can send me to the right room, the right shelf, at an instant. The only real difficulty lies with the prolific sinners like Hemingway, who qualify for several different categories, and there I make value judgments, and rely on mnemonics." The old man took a deep breath, licked his aged lips with a tongue that to her eyes insanely resembled the head of a slug exploring the crack in a sidewalk for nutrients, and said, "Would you like to hear how I knew where to look for Charlotte Winsborough?"

Amber had heard of a method, possibly only an urban legend, that some hunters reputedly use to capture monkeys. It involved placing a fruit inside the knot-hole of a tree. The monkey reaches in and grabs the treat, but with it in his grasp, his fist is too large to be withdrawn. He cannot bring himself to drop the treasure in his possession, and so he remains trapped, in *its* possession, for however long it takes the clever hunter to return with a net. Here with this demented old man, this close to terrible knowledge about the author who had come to consume her academic life, Amber could have demurred and walked out without the dread knowledge that was now being offered to her. But it was impossible, not with the secret within her grasp, and a little voice inside her asked, forlornly, if the monkeys ever understood the nature of the trap that had imprisoned them. So she remained where she was, and said nothing.

The old man said, "I happen to know something about Charlotte Winsborough that she only told one other person in her entire life, when she was in her eighties and no longer writing, an invalid looking Death in the eye and fearing that none of the good she'd done in her life would ever save her from an eternity in Hell.

"She made her confession to a young caregiver on the condition of absolute secrecy, but of course that caregiver wasted no time at all telling a friend, who many years later shared it in a letter to her cousin, as an interesting anecdote. She did not represent her story as fascinating trivia about a famous writer, because she was not herself someone who cared for books at all, and would not have retained the information that the old woman had ever written any.

"The amount of research I required to uncover this information would fill a book all by itself, but obtaining information of that sort has always been my true avocation, and obtaining it about living authors, especially best-sellers, who happily pay to keep it confidential, has been a steady income stream even in this sadly post-literate age. It's why I don't get to read as many of my acquisitions as I would like, but at the very least, it supports this house, and makes a collection of this sort possible.

"What I know, Amber, is that Charlotte Winsborough once murdered an infant.

"No, please; you may not want to believe it, but I assure you that I have all the documentation I require. It happened when she was twenty-six, an unmarried woman in an era when that qualified her as a spinster, trapped with an invalid mother in a country house. The great love of her life, the good man she wrote about many years later in her memoir *The Orchard*, was still ahead of her. But she was not at that early point, as her biographers to date and, I believe likely yourself, have tended to believe, a repressed virgin. She'd already had a quite healthy sex life, if a furtive one, maintaining relationships with lovers who during this specific period included a married pillar of the community whose own wife was frigid. I have the man's letters to Charlotte in an off-site storage facility where I keep all such documentation, providing further evidence supporting the great confession Charlotte made late in life: that he impregnated her and refused responsibility.

"Despite her own failing health and the degree to which she depended on her downtrodden daughter for her every need, Charlotte's mother, a cruel and judgmental harridan who terrorized and dominated her, only barely tolerated her daughter's literary career, at this point only one self-published book of poetry, as a foolish affectation. To her, writing was something that no respectable person, let alone a decent woman, would ever do, and she would have put a stop to it had she possessed any belief that Charlotte would ever enjoy any real success at the endeavor. So Charlotte, who at that point in her life could envision no possibility of escaping her circumstances, existed in considerable fear even before she first sensed the changes in her own body and understood what they meant. Once this additional danger reared itself, she knew that if her mother ever found out she would be banished from their house, disinherited, and driven out of town. Her few options while penniless would have included prostitution: a fate Charlotte's mother would have considered fitting, and not all that far removed from that earlier sin, literature while female.

"Charlotte, a hefty woman by today's anorexic standards, and one granted additional camouflage by the voluminous clothing of her time, hid her pregnancy. She ate little to minimize the attendant baby bump, endured her mother's insults about the weight that still accrued, and one cold February night stuffed a rag in her mouth and endured the agonies of labor in silence.

"So successful was she at hiding the birth that the hateful old woman down the hall heard almost nothing. Her later confession to her own young caregiver included the detail that mother did indeed hear the one cry made by the little girl, and shouted a demand for an explanation. But the old woman was mollified by Charlotte's shouted reply that the cry had just been herself, waking from a bad dream. This made sense, given the hour: sometime between two and three AM. It would be the only sound the little girl made before Charlotte smothered her, to prevent any further incriminating cries. Within only a few hours, the obscure poet and future temporarily important novelist had recovered enough from her physical ordeal, and from the tears attendant in what she had done, to pop in on her mother and say that she was heading outside to tend to one of her regular chores, chopping wood. A tough woman, Charlotte was, pioneer stock you might say, though according to her confession what she chopped to pieces on that day was nothing quite as hard to section as lumber. The pieces went into the pond.

"And that's it, really. Charlotte kept this secret all her life, ultimately marrying a respectable man who trusted her claims of virginity, and having two daughters who lived full if ordinary lives without ever suffering the touch of the axe. She kept her terrible secret for decades, only for that secret to pass, as so many have, into the hands of this humble book curator, who was, with that, empowered to shelve her literary work in the special category of authors who had murdered small children. There are enough of these, Amber, that I have had to further divide that category into number of victims, and respective ages; and you would be stunned indeed by some of the names, genuinely stunned. I needed repairs to the roof, not long ago, and was able to able to get the expense underwritten by another name you would recognize, a very wealthy lady still alive whose multiple editions are shelved not far from Charlotte's . . . but there, dear Amber, I start to ramble. You've come a long way. I'm sure you'll need to be getting back."

He handed Amber the bag containing her purchase, and as she took it with trembling hands, the brown paper crinkled. To her it did not resemble a sound made by paper, but rather the guttural rumble of a predator, when it is steeling itself for a kill. And yet it was still just a crinkle, backed by the hard surface of a book printed on the other side of the world.

He said, "I look forward to your dissertation."

She thanked him, accepted his offer of a business card, and showed herself out. Once back in the open air, far from the scent of paper, she hurried down the well-kept walk, got in her car, and sat in it for eight and a half minutes, her hands on the wheel, and her eyes staring at the road ahead, before she finally turned the key and finally left the estate grounds. She drove at a measured rate, slower than she usually did, but did manage to get back to campus housing before dark.

In the morning she alerted the school that she had decided to abandon her studies, effective immediately. She would not publish, would in fact not add even one more word to her dissertation. She said that her life priorities had changed and that she would have to find some other endeavor to occupy herself. When she informed the professor who had sent her to the collector of rare books, the woman did not seem particularly surprised; she indeed possessed the demeanor of someone who had expected precisely this response. After a token attempt to talk Amber out of this life decision, she extended her hand and wished the departing student well. But was there a predatory, triumphant glint in those eyes? Amber could not tell.

In any event, Amber left town, heading for a future that does not concern us. On her way she was sometimes weeping and sometimes suicidal, and often she was just grim-faced, but she was also sometimes giddy with the relief known to soldiers when the battle is done and they are among the few still left standing.

The problem had not been that she'd been shattered by the crime of Charlotte Winsborough.

Amber was an adult who knew as much as she had to know about Charlotte's era, who understood that such things had gone on, then, and still went on, now. The old man had given her biographical details she hadn't known, but none of it had been enough to break her, not all by itself. That wasn't the problem.

It was only that Amber knew herself even more intimately than she knew the woman whose career had been the focus of all that wasted scholarship.

And she knew just where her completed dissertation would have been shelved.

THE LAST TO MATTER

Kayn knew he was being rejected by the orgynism for almost a full year before it fully expelled him.

He could easily live a million years past this humiliation and never understand what he had done to deserve such a rejection from the collective that had loved him so well, for so long.

He had been one of the orgynism's founders, the man who had provided its organizing principles and solicited the first participants, the architect who had drawn up the parameters for the pleasure-feedback loops, and as a result, he'd been honored to spend its many years of existence as the seed nexus around which all its carnality orbited. For all that time, the orgynism's participants, male and female and neuter and recombinant, had always tithed some of their pleasure to his, their sensations flowing in his direction through the neural connections all had agreed to upon joining the collective, just as their other surgically implanted connections also provided him with oxygen for his lungs and nutrients for his blood. Pierced in all of a dozen places and piercing in a dozen others, he had known nothing but mindless bliss, at the orgynism's core.

How lucky he had considered himself, at those rare moments when conscious thought had space to intervene, for living in a time when such things were possible!

One would think that the bastards would have damn well appreciated that.

Then, one by one, the connections were withdrawn, the devotion toward his pleasure above all else was sidelined, and the peristalsis of the dozens of interconnected bodies began to move him, bit by bit, toward the outskirts. The limbs of his many lovers now grasped him not in embrace but in firm urging toward the exit, and though they were gentle about it, taking more than a year to shift him from the orgynism's center to its periphery, they also brooked no argument. He continued to feel pleasure. But, throughout, he also knew that he was being dispensed with.

At the end of the year, Kayn popped sweaty and glistening from the hovering sphere of bodies, and slammed to the soft floor a man-height below. The living tubes that had provided him with nutrients and euphoric drugs tore free of his flesh and slithered back into the ball of copulating bodies, there to disappear beneath the shifting landscape of shoulders and buttocks and ecstatic faces. Nobody whose features were exposed bothered to open their eyes and acknowledge his bereft status, his enforced farewell; not one of the women, not one of the men, not any of the recombinants said goodbye. As far as they were concerned, he was gone, and he was forgotten, as irrelevant to the orgynism as any other sight or sound of the world its pleasures locked out.

For some time, he sat moist and heartbroken below the throbbing ball of former lovers, lost in the novelty of separation. Then a portal opened on the wall to his right and his replacement, a creature with a half-dozen sets of complete sexual organs from forehead to midriff, undulated in, its naked form already studded with the necessary interfaces for the nutrient tubes and neurological feedback wires. It glanced at him, registering his predicament but not remarking on it, before turning away and striding the rest of the way to the orgynism Kayn had left and that it was now joining. One leap and the new lover was caught. The orgynism throbbed at the point of impact, and swallowed the newcomer whole.

Kayn considered fighting his way back into the collective, clawing with tooth and nail back to a dominant place at its center. But as dev-astated as he was, he knew that this would be a pathetic and doomed attempt at rape. He'd be outnumbered, for one thing. For another, now that not all of his consciousness was dominated by incoming sensation, the emptiness of the rutting that had occupied so many years of his life depressed him. Maybe that's why his lovers had expelled him; they'd sensed his flagging commitment.

So he stood. He applied to the same portal the newcomer had entered for his own exit, passing through the surgical vestibule now tasked with rendering him respectable for the outside world. It first sprayed him with topical anesthetics, and then with flashes of whirring knives amputated the various extra sexual inlets and protuberances that he'd needed before but would not be using again, a dizzying flurry of male and female castrations and other surgeries coupled with accelerated healing that by the time he'd completed ten steps had restored him to his birth settings. As soon as he was whole, spray nozzles emerged from the walls, bathed him, and then covered him with a thin gloss of purple liquid that congealed as neck-to-ankle clothing. It was not clothing in the sense that it preserved modesty, in part because he had none; it simply conformed to the shape of his genitalia, displaying it in full openness as was only proper. It was also imbedded with connections to the machines that did all the city's thinking, which anticipated his likely needs and informed him that there were currently still seventeen other orgynisms being maintained at various other locations around the city. Some were currently recruiting. He could resume his carnal pleasures with scarcely a pause for the gathering of breath. But the paucity of this number shocked him. When he founded his orgynism, there'd been more than three hundred others. Thirteen of the seventeen still in existence were full up, their participants having opted for full lobotomization in order to fight off any urges toward disbanding. Four had heard about his ejection, and had issued invitations to his account. He demurred and moved on. The door at the end of the vestibule slid into its recess and provided the newly-freed, freshly-clothed, sexually-refreshed Kayn back onto the street.

He composed a sonnet of heartbreak. He did this in the way anybody had written anything, in the last few millennia: by taking it upon himself to declare that such a thing should be written and mentally ordering the machines that ran everything to write one for him. It was produced at once, delivered to his cortex by the connection with the machines that was the birthright of all who lived.

What emerged was the worst sonnet ever.

He was no expert in poetry. Nobody was. That was why composing it had long since become the domain of the machines. Who wanted to go to all that effort, especially since no one would ever read it? Might as well let the machines take care of that impulse. But in past years, they would have come up with a *good* sonnet. This one was mostly made-up words, and still failed to scan.

How irritating.

He didn't order a replacement. He just set about finding out what had become of the city during his years of distraction.

· · · ·

Once, there had been tens of thousands of cities. They had hugged the shorelines and punctuated the rivers and marked the wider points in the road, wherever goods were carried from one place to another. They had occupied the places where the holes were dug in the earth so the resources could be ripped out; places where the crops were grown, where the tools were built, even where people went just to lay in the sun. Once there had been enough people to fill those tens of thousands of cities. Then many had fled Earth, launching themselves at a universe that seemed infinite with possibility. A few had come back saying that this had turned out not to be true, that the universe was in fact a cold and inhospitable place with little soil congenial to humanity; a few others had returned and said that this was nonsense, that the stars teemed with opportunities for those who possessed the courage to seize them, and that humanity's diaspora had accomplished wonders undreamt of by those who had stayed behind. Either story could have been true. But it no longer mattered which, now. Eons had passed. The distant outposts had fallen silent. The constellations had gone dark. Most civilization had crumbled to dust. The descendants of the billions who stayed behind had dwindled to millions, and then to thousands.

Long before Kayn joined the orgynism, the city had shrunk in the ways cities do when there are no longer enough people to fill them. Entire sections had been claimed by the surrounding desert, even as others were built up to look more elaborate, more magnificent, more a play-palace for the residents who remained. When Kayn founded his orgynism, one could still venture out into the remaining streets and find a crowd, at any hour of the day or night (those being antiquated distinctions even by then, as the sun no longer shone brightly enough to make a proper day). But sometime since he first joined his lovers, the city's masses had thinned out even more. Even on the first major thoroughfare Kayn investigated, there were almost no people, except for those who had elected to become trees and who stood at regular intervals, being watered by automatic systems, as they spread their arms and faced a sky that reflected their emptiness with its own.

Some of the trees could still talk and provided him with directions, an important service when the streets had changed orientation and no longer led to the right places, but they were trees and not capable of much conversation beyond that. So Kayn headed for the city center, where there was always activity to be had, and as he went he ran into some of his remaining neighbors.

He met a dandy being fitted for a suit more magnificent than any ever produced by any tailor. It was a glossy multi-colored thing that, the dandy told him, the mechanisms had been laboring to spin on his frame for several decades now. It was far too voluminous to permit physical movement and so the dandy sat at the center of enough frilled cloth to fill a space the size of a ballroom, only his face showing, like an egg being cradled by an acre of satin. Hand-mirrors orbited him, propelled by little puffs of compressed air that also served to dispense perfume. "I am beautiful," he told Kayn. "I am the most beautiful thing alive." It was his ambition to have fresh frills added to his ever-growing outfit for as long as the machines remained sufficiently operational to do so, at which point he would have himself injected with a plasticizing compound so he could spend what remained of eternity as his suit's undecaying mannequin. Kayn commended him on his choice of performance art and moved on.

He met a woman who had decided to spend her years giving birth. She sat naked, her back against a wall, her legs splayed to facilitate the escape of her offspring, a glistening fetal something who while Kayn watched several times squirmed its way free of her birth canal, then climbed up her body to force its way back into her open mouth. This was its cyclical journey: escaping her, then escaping the outside world, then escaping her again. The woman was unable to tell Kayn why she'd chosen to spend her years this way, likely because her child's constant invasions of her throat had ravaged her vocal cords, but the baby had the consciousness of an adult and was able to tell Kayn what it knew of the city's recent history. There'd been some programmed revolutions, some happy genocides, the rise of some murderous despot or two who had painted the streets with blood until the city decreed that it was no longer their turn to have fun. Once, a murderer had been brought in, and the citizenry had amused itself being slaughtered by him. This, Kayn figured, accounted for much of the fallen population. But the baby informed him of something else that also made sense, given the squalor of the cityscape around him: that the machines that kept things running had been breaking down for years, and that as more and more of them stopped working, the servitors were only able to keep some neighborhoods running by scavenging parts from those that didn't. Kayn took this with some excitement. He was starving for novelty and found being part of a crumbling civilization just what he needed. He thanked the baby for its time and moved on.

He passed a circular fountain, now dry and caked with clotted blood, where the skeletons of two human beings lay in a heap that suggested they'd died together. An old man sat throwing bread crumbs on the bodies, in order to enjoy the sight of the birds fluttering around the bones. Kayn asked what had happened and the old man said that there were any number of sights like this, tucked in this place and that: evidence of that killer who had been allowed to run amuck for a while, for the entertainment value that provided. Kayn, who had been murdered once or twice in his long life and did not care to have that happen again, asked if the pet killer had been disposed of once his novelty value was exhausted, and the old man said, "Oh, sure, sure; really, there's only so much you can do with a creature like that, before they start to repeat themselves in unacceptable ways." He sighed, pointed at the larger of the two skeletons and said, "That one was me." Kayn bid the old man farewell and moved further into the center of the city, finding along the way that he had to traverse any number of places where passages were blocked by drifts of sand.

This is how he knew that he was getting closer to the place he sought.

· · · ·

In outline the city resembled the infinity symbol, a pair of teardrop-shapes designed to converge at the narrowest points. This deliberate bottleneck was an intersection less than a hundred paces across at its narrowest point, open to the untouched landscape on both sides. It was a feature originally designed as a place of wonder, a plaza where the citizenry could pause and take in the unspoiled, or at least unpopulated, wilderness outside the city walls, reflect on the part of the world no one in the city ever needed, and move on, to whatever pleasures awaited in either of their home's two halves.

The last time Kayn had been to this place, just before joining with the orgynism, the mechanisms that had kept the desert on both sides from intruding on this narrow bottleneck of civilization had already started to fail, and the pavement tiles had all felt gritty underfoot, a first sign that the sands had already begun to intrude. It was worse now. The drifts of gray sand now extended from one side of the narrow strip to another, fingers of pure decay well into the process of sundering the city's two halves from one another. In the very center, the tiles had disintegrated completely, and Kayn did not just stumble over shifting sands but sink knee-deep into them. Something bit him in the leg. He cursed and dragged himself onto the tiles on the other side of the gap, pulling the buried creature along with him: He yanked it free of his leg, and examined the thing that had bitten him at arm's length. It was a tiny thing as wide as his wrist, with a nearly human face but for the slit nose and lipless mouth, and little human arms, but a torso that trailed to a point rather than sprout legs. Everything below its waist looked like some turds do, when they've been inside the colon so long that they've taken on the wrinkles and folds of the surrounding tissue.

Kayn almost smashed the shit-thing dead, but then it said, "Don't kill me!"

He grimaced but did not hurl it away as he would have wanted. "What are you?"

"I'm a man."

Kayn said, "I don't believe you."

"Laugh all you want. I'm prepared for when the city's gone. I'll survive a lot longer than you. I'll still be thriving in these sands when the sun goes cold."

Blood, Kayn's blood, dripped from the thing's fangs.

Kayn said, "The sun's gone cold. It made the news."

"Colder," the shit-thing clarified. "If it had gone out, we'd all be dead."

"Cold enough. The desert won't support life."

"You're half-right. It won't support *human* life. You can't go stumbling out there, trying to make a go of it, without freezing your nuts off. But life like me is still making a go of it, and will for a while yet. I'm the wave of the future. So feed me or let me go; I'm tired of your crap."

Kayn almost hurled it to the tiles and stomped it to a greasy spot, but there are penalties to casual murder even in a city where murder can be arranged as a source of entertainment, and so he simply dropped it into the gap between the city's decaying halves, and watched as it burrowed its way into the sands. He wondered if it was alone or if it was one member of a thriving colony, and if so, just what they fed on, down there, as it could not survive only on the blood of those like him, who stumbled in the crossing. And then he shrugged. In any city, even this one, it was possible to intercept any number of stories that had nothing to do with yourself, and if you did not want them to become your stories instead, you had to move on, banishing them to the status of footnotes or apocrypha.

He marched on, past the narrows, past a broken archway into the city's other half, where after a while he began encountering other residents again. An emaciated but bearded woman, clad only in the few strips of clothing that had not yet rotted off her, nodded at him as she crossed an avenue, bearing a squirming human-shaped something in a sack on her shoulders. Two children, a rarity when he'd joined the orgynism, sat in a tree chattering nonsense at one another, and he spent a few minutes attempting to coax them down before realizing that, human or not, they were joined to the tree by stems, and enjoying life as its fruit. A man in a long multi-colored coat, ragged and bearded and mad, darted into a narrow alley lined with knives, that ripped pieces from him as he fled heedless into a potent darkness at its other end. Two other men played a variant of chess, only with many thousands of additional pawns and knights, across a game board so vast that their pieces had yet to contend with one another at the center of the board; both players were draped in drifts of dust, each one so involved in calculating the possible ramifications of any move that it might have been years since they had done anything but wait.

* * * *

It was only after he entered a neighborhood where none of the buildings had doors, where they were just unmarked monoliths offering no clue as to what they might have contained, that he found a place that had been once been one of his favorites. Prior civilizations would have called it an inn, or café, or restaurant. It served the same function with some adjustments for the nature of the way the city's people interacted with one another. The last time he'd been here, centuries earlier, had been Poison Day and he had sat alongside two dozen other patrons there to soak up the novelty of dining and dying and dining and dying only to dine and die some more. It had been glorious. Today, of course, he didn't want to feel his insides turn to fire inside him. He just wanted to plug himself back into whatever social intercourse the city could still provide, while making contacts for whatever grand joy came next. And so he entered the familiar room with its frescoes of hanging gardens, overjoyed to find it, if not full, then at least occupied by half a dozen others, including two old men locked in conversation, one lone man addressing his soup with what could only be described as grim determination, and a forlorn young woman with dark circles under her eyes, staring at her plate of something as if wholly uncertain what it was.

Kayn said, "Excuse me."

The woman was silver-skinned, no doubt plated with the actual metal, a fashion choice that had been popular once upon a time. He supposed that it must be completely antiquarian now. So were her eyes, which were pink and lemur-large against cheeks buffed to a mirrored finish. She sat with her delicate hands palm-down on the table, flanking her bowl but making no move to lift it to her lips. But she was not forlorn enough to ignore Kayn's hello. She met his gaze and released half-a-dozen syllables of purest gibberish in no language he knew, which was not all that unusual. Kayn had lived through entire renaissances of enthused linguistic experimentation where all of the city's thousands had ordered the machines to design individual tongues for them, and had happily wandered the streets as citizens of Babel, content to not understand each other at all.

He pressed further: "Do you understand me?"

She cycled through a dozen tongues, some known to him, and some not, before arriving at the one he'd used to address her. "Can I help you?"

"Will you accept my company?"

"I wasn't looking for company, but I don't specifically object to it. I am willing to discuss anything but politics, morality, or the flattening effect of multiplying temporal paradoxes."

"My full name is Adam Splendor Sadness Feline Igneous Ultimate Never Cul-De-Sac Untoward Synchronicity Leverage Cystic Beverage Arrogance Wholly Thirteen Cunnilingus Hummingbird Multiplication Kayn. You can call me Kayn."

She provided her name, not a spoken syllable but a blast of tropical warmth, humid and filled with peat. "You can call me Peat. Please sit."

"All right." He sat opposite her, and let the table generate a meal for him, utensils and all. There was no mucking about with menus, sentient or otherwise. The establishment had tasted him and determined just what combination of foodstuffs was most appropriate for his current mood. What came, rising out of the solid table like the sun coming up on the horizon, was a bowl of something moving, something clearly sentient and alive, something that sang in soft, mournful despair as it awaited slaughter at the tip of his heated, six-pronged fork. He didn't make it wait for very long, just stabbed through its tiny skull with one ruthless thrust, and lifted it to his mouth, feeling satiated as its death throes distributed what flavor it had. This had long been one of his favorite dishes. But today it was oily and bland, and when he was done chewing, it left an unpleasant gritty residue between his teeth. It was as if the sand of the surrounding desert had gotten into the synthesizers themselves.

She noted his displeasure and said, "You're surprised. You must have been gone for a while. Orgynism?"

"Yes."

"I was in one, about eight hundred years ago. It was a big one, with over a thousand participants, at its peak. It was bliss until one near the center went insane and started chewing his way out. I'm still missing some toes. How long have you been out?"

He told her.

"That explains your reaction to the food. You're new to the way things have been falling apart."

"I notice you're not eating either."

"I never do. I have no stomach. No internal organs of any kind. This," she said, drumming her silvery digits on the table, "is what I'm made of now. I suppose I'll last longer this way, when the city's gone."

"So it's not a rumor."

"No."

He pointed at her food. "You ordered."

"I wanted to sit. The table provided. But I outgrew food long ago. You should, too. The city won't be making much more of it."

He remembered the predictions of the shit-thing. "How much time do you think we still have? Months? Years? Centuries?"

"Who cares? It's not like this place is fun anymore. We've seen everything. We've done everything. I'm only alive out of inertia."

He said, "Up for suicide? I'll join you, if that's what you want."

"I've done that," Peat replied. "It didn't take."

"Then let's get married."

"I've done that a couple of dozen times, too. Once with you, in fact, though we weren't the only people involved. But if you'd like to be in love for a while, just to pass the time, I'm willing to do that."

"All right," said Kayn.

Their courtship over, they both left the table, to make the necessary arrangements.

* * * *

They didn't know each other and didn't like each other much, but that was no longer an inconvenience, not when they were both available and there were still working machines dispensing love. It was just a matter of recalibrating their internal referents and setting what intensity they wanted, from mild affection to all-out raging, clothes-shredding passion. The first through fourth of the stations they investigated were all derelict, three merely devoid of power and one incapable of producing anything but flatulent noises, but the fifth they found, in a vacant bazaar on the seventh level of the abandoned Third Church of Gilgul the Materialist, was still capable of producing Love at some settings, albeit none of the better ones. As per his lifelong habit as a man more comfortable with receiving that emotion than feeling it, he took a dose two notches lower than hers, and felt a surge of deep affection while she elected to feel something more, something rich and genuine and pure.

There was no chance of a standard honeymoon night, not that he wanted one, after the sexual surfeit of his recent centuries. He may have still possessed the parts, but she did not. But companionship, she provided. They shared a bed and sometimes a vat, and during the days they wandered the city, noting all the places that still existed and those that were still a ghost of what they had used to be.

They went to the Cinema, the last Cinema, a place that had been established millennia before, where mechanisms behind the screen projected a perpetual story compelling enough to be joined or abandoned at any point, without any sense that one had missed something. Alas, something primal had been lost over the years. In Kayn's youth, the story had been an intricate saga of intrigue in the court of some medieval kingdom, driven by subtle turns of character and shifts of power dynamics among a cast of thousands. It had once kept him in his seat, being fed and tended by bots, for more than a month before the sameness overwhelmed him and he'd wandered out of the auditorium looking for a place to set some bombs. Years later, he'd returned, and the story had contracted to two men, armed with knives, grappling with one another in the center of a field of corpses. He'd spent a day watching them cut little strips of flesh off one another's bodies, discerned no story, and left. Now, returning with Peat to an auditorium ankle-deep in sand occupied by a half-dozen dusty patrons he recognized from his earlier visits and who he presumed to have been watching the entire saga from the beginning, he found that the story had contracted still further: It was now a man forever punching a solid wall with the wrist-nubs that were all that remained of his arms, after his fists had eroded from an unimaginable number of constant impacts. "The machines are stuck," Peat explained. "They used to be able to introduce new characters, establish new plot developments, create brand-new complications capable of carrying the narrative to new places, but in recent years they've been deteriorating. The narrative's become fossilized. You can sit for years waiting for something different to happen."

"It's a great unintentional metaphor," said Kayn.

The two of them stayed six hours, just watching the unfortunate on screen pummel the wall, waiting for something else to happen, anything else to happen. Nothing did, and they ultimately left in search of new adventures.

They found an abandoned building where Peat said that she'd lived once, a tower now leaning seventeen degrees which once would have been righted or had its architectural deficiency incorporated as a fresh source of novelty, and scaled the exterior to the summit, one hundred and forty stories above the avenue below. The apartment they found there was infested with spiders, and criss-crossed with vast curtains of webbing. The tenants, three women and one man, were cocooned and in the process of being digested, but did not seem to mind. One explained to Kayn that the spiders made such wonderful music. Kayn could detect nothing. Peat said that she could: "It's just above your range of hearing, Kayn."

He asked her what kind of music they were playing, and she said: "Waltzes. I can hum along, if you'd like to dance." So they danced, the tightly wrapped residents of the apartment watching with delight and fascination as Kayn and Peat spun their circles across the tilted floor. How long they danced, Kayn could not tell, but it was long enough for the spiders to begin the process of capturing them, swathing Kayn in what looked like bandages and Peat in what looked like a diaphanous gown. And for a while he thought that it would not be a bad thing for his years of existence to end this way, so high above the city streets, as close to the dimming stars as he had ever been. But the spiders began to work in earnest, his skin began to itch, and he was moved to tell Peat that maybe they ought to go. They climbed back down, without him hearing so much as a single note.

Back on the streets, they found a corpse willing to speak to them. Terrible things had been done to him by a passing murderer of unremitting savagery, perhaps the same one whose handiwork Kayn had already seen here and there: It honestly didn't matter, not to the victim and not to Kayn, because the deed had been done and the corpse was not willing to do anything constructive to fix it. His chest was still open to the elements, but he had elected not to heal or to die, but rather to continue to lie where the monster had left him, choosing to spend what time the city had left on his back, in contemplation of the few remaining stars. He said, "I remember being part of a great love story. I do not remember whether it was two men or two women or one woman and one man or a pair of thirders or any of the hundreds of other possible combinations we came up with, by the time it all started falling apart, but I remember being one of them. I remember telling the one I loved that I would never forget. I remember the finger against my lips, the whispered words, sure you will; everything we have done is just footnote. That turned out to be true. It was the one great love of my life and it happened so long ago that I cannot remember who my lover was, or for that matter who I was. I just remember regretting that I went on after it ended." He took a deep breath that caused the cavity at the center of his chest to bubble, and then spoke with special urgency: "The city's going to fall."

"We know that," said Peat.

The murdered man said, "I don't mean millennia from now. I don't mean centuries from now, or even any span of years. I mean weeks or months, no more. Listen: We're sinking. Listen: We will soon be swallowed up. Listen: The sand will come in and fill the streets and blot out the sky and scour everything clean. Listen: Anybody who stays will die. Anybody who wants to live must leave."

Kayn had already reached this conclusion just by walking around, but he had seen the dune sea: a desert that had long ago spread worldwide, without any fantastical oases or lands untouched by the entropy that had overtaken everything else. "There's no place to go."

The corpse could only repeat himself. "Anybody who wants to live must leave."

"Shush, shush," said Peat. She pressed a mirrored fingertip to the corpse's lips, burning them slightly because of the generated heat she could do nothing to tamp. Being a corpse, he felt nothing but the intended comfort, and he grew calm long enough for her to speak the only ameliorating truth she could. "There's no reason to worry. Nobody here wants to live, anyway."

• • • •

Later, Kayn said, "But I do want to live."

By now they were wandering through one of the last remaining libraries with books made of paper. It was, not, of course, real paper, made from trees: that would have deteriorated to dust long before. Paper had not been a thing since all information was trusted to the machines, and before that, since any texts human beings might still have some purpose for had been transferred to silicates. These books were designed to feel like paper, but were made of flexible alloys, chemically inert and designed to last forever. What a pity that some past vandal had seen fit to black out every line of type with a pigment just as eternal as the pages themselves, before re-shelving them in cases of the same material, as a means of ensuring that their splendid meaninglessness lasted forever!

He made his pronouncement while Peat was running her silvery hands over the pages of one volume grabbed at random, just to enjoy its texture. She looked up and said, "What?"

He repeated himself. "I do want to live."

"But everything's ending."

"I don't care. I haven't done everything I wanted to do. I haven't seen everything I wanted to see. I don't want this story to be over. I want to keep adding to it. I want to live past the point where there's any point in living."

She was aghast. "Why?"

"I don't know."

"I've watched you. You're as bored as I am. As bored as everyone is."

"I can't deny it."

"Then why would you want this to go on?"

"I don't know. I think it's a birth defect of some kind."

"There are no birth defects. The machines can fix any flaw there is."

"I have one. I don't seem to be able to give up."

She said, "You implanted love for me. You can implant a death wish. It's just as simple. There must be some machine still capable of doing that."

"I tried that, years ago. Before the orgynism. I thought the time had come to end myself. I couldn't make myself want to. I went to one of the machines and told it to adjust me, to make me content with the time I had lived, and ready to stop. It made noise for a while and then stopped. It was non-functional. Something about me had broken it. I tried another machine and then a third, with identical results. I broke down every machine I asked. When I realized it was impossible, I decided that blissful oblivion was just as good, and started recruiting lovers for my orgynism." He thought about it for a while, as driven to silence by her nonplussed reaction as she was to what he said, and reported, "I don't know. Maybe that's why the orgynism rejected me. But I want to live. I'm stuck that way."

She flipped through some more pages, caressing each one she stopped at, finding nothing new on any of them, but still finding mild distraction with the way they felt.

Then she said, "I don't think I can love anyone so old-fashioned."

• • • •

They didn't break up right away. Just as heat takes time to dissipate, so does affection, and so they spent the next few days having other shared adventures, some romantic and some not, as a means of continuing to spend the time that was now in such short supply.

They found a building on the edge of a neighborhood that had already been reclaimed by the sands, with one collapsed wing and one that seemed to remain upright only out of sheer stubbornness. It was an orphanage, long-abandoned, and the bottom floor was a nursery filled with babies. They were manufactured children, grown in vats and tended by servitors like all the world's children had been, since long before this was the only city. Aged to what the peak age of what once would have been considered appealing, they were forever frozen at that level of maturity to be claimed by whatever adoptive parents happened to show up. There had of course been none for a long time, and thus every crib being tended had an occupant, squirming and cooing beneath inches of dust. There was no point in taking any of them, and so Kayn and Peat just spent an hour or so wandering among the bassinets, neither oohing nor aahing, but not immune to the pathos either. They named the cutest one, the one they would have taken had they been in the market, "Forever." Forever regarded them with interest, imprinting. This, given their dearth of interest, was probably not a favor.

They found a machine in the shape of a pulsating sphincter attended by a tarnished servitor who explained that it was an art installation, designed to turn things into other things. Any object placed within the loading portal would be devoured and shat out the other side as another object entirely. Peat had seen such merriments before but Kayn had not, and so she stood by indulgently as he tested its capabilities with the various artifacts in range. He gave the orifice a stone plucked from the borders of a wilted garden, and watched as the orifice sucked it in, chewed, and produced an obscene statue of a woman having sexual congress with a tree. He gave it a little wooden table from an abandoned nearby café, and watched as the mastication produced a mound of broken glass. Then he ordered the servitor to feed itself to the orifice, and, being a machine, it obeyed without protest. The orifice chewed and the thing that came out the back was alive and boneless and incapable of any action but unending screams.

Peat said, "That was interesting."

Kayn felt bad for the servitor, which had been polite and unoffending and didn't deserve an end of this sort. Maybe feeding it to the orifice would produce an improvement? Perhaps, but it could also produce something much worse, and so he ended up doing nothing.

They sought out warmth, in the form of the city's last furnace, a raging open conflagration that Kayn could not approach but that Peat was able to enter and explore, without harm. Her silvery flesh did not melt but grew red-hot, a transformation that rendered her so beautiful that Kayn might have fallen in love with her all over again, without artificial assistance. She spun and danced and sang, an ember that, for a few minutes, looked like she might have been able to devour all that remained of the city, all by herself. She seemed joyous. But once she left, she cooled rapidly, both in temperature and in mood, and she said, "That, on the other hand, was boring. I think I've decided to die now."

"Are you sure? Maybe you'll feel better in the morning."

"Who wants to feel better? I've *done* that."

Kayn could not dissuade her, and so they spent her last night in a ballroom that had become only a little shabbier over the centuries, dancing tangos and waltzes and pretending for a while to be a great lord and lady from one of those past eras that still had such things. At midnight an artificial moon rose on the other side of the crushed stained-glass windows, casting a beam of multicolored wonder through the dusty air. He kissed her for the first and only time, a moment of contact between his flesh and whatever her flesh happened to be that felt too much like kissing a thing made of ice. She said, "Goodbye," disentangled herself from his arms, and strode to the center of the dance floor, raising one graceful arm and standing en pointe in a spot where her many shiny surfaces could reflect the moonbeam to every corner of the hall. It seemed like a moment of perfect stillness in the middle of a ballet. But as the long seconds passed, and she never came out of it, Kayn saw that she wasn't going to. He approached her and touched a finger to her metallic cheek, finding a nub just below her right eye that might have been a metallic tear, and confirmed that whatever had made her Peat was gone.

• • • •

He wandered for a few weeks after that, interacting with as many of the city's fading wonders as he could, but found fewer that worked and even fewer that he had not seen.

When he had decided that, he fell into revisiting some of the places where he had already been.

He went to the nursery, found Forever—who was already gathering a new layer of dust—held him for a little bit, and said some things about connections that fail and times that end, that Forever must have understood not at all.

He went to the library, gazed upon all the shelves lined with unreadable books, and stood for a while in the presence of all those unknowable narratives, and contemplated a life spent curled up with them, the life he would have been happy enough to undertake were it possible to cross the obstructions between those words and his eyes.

He revisited the murdered man, who told him again that things were ending and that there was no time to lose, if he wanted to live.

He went back to the Cinema to see where the story had gone, and found that it had indeed progressed since his last visit. The image on screen was no longer a man punching a wall, but was now a different man, one who looked very much like Kayn himself, sitting cross-legged in a desert very much like the one currently engulfing the city. The man was alive and aware and clearly capable of action; it was possible to tell, just from the way he blinked at the moments when one errant breeze or another deposited grains of sand in his eyes. But he did nothing to shield himself, nothing to rescue himself from the forces that would soon enough bury him. He was spent. And in the fourth hour that Kayn spent absorbed in this absence of all adventure, the star of the movie shifted, turned his dusty visage toward the audience, and focused on Kayn alone, ignoring the handful of others who had sitting for far longer, waiting for him to do something worth seeing.

He said, "Go."

Kayn said, "Where?"

"I don't care, Adam Splendor Sadness Feline Igneous Ultimate Never Cul-De-Sac Untoward Synchronicity Leverage Cystic Beverage Arrogance Wholly Thirteen Cunnilingus Hummingbird Multiplication Kayn. This show is over for you. Go elsewhere."

Kayn, who had never been the type to stay where he wasn't wanted, went.

He retraced all his steps, lingering here and there and taking weeks for the journey, until he found himself back in the room of his greatest humiliation, looking up at what was left of his old orgynism, and found that it had deteriorated horribly in his absence. No longer an approximate sphere, it was now a crescent moon, disfigured by a great gaping crater where fully a third of the participants had either been pushed out, or had left of their own accord. Of those who remained, only about half were still in motion, attempting to make up with their efforts what the immobile remainder no longer could. Their union no longer looked like bliss, but like desperation, denial of that which was coming for all of them. One of those still grinding away, but not looking at all well, opened his eyes and noticed Kayn. He said, "I suppose you came to gloat."

"No," said Kayn. "I did not."

"Liar! I know the way it works! You want us to say that it all fell to pieces when you left! Well, it did, but you had nothing to do with it! It was an inevitability, a shift in our corporeal paradigm, that was only the next natural step in the evolution of our union! Soon, we will re-incorporate under new principles and achieve heights we never would have known were we still with you, slaves to your antiquated erotic philosophy! We would not have you back even if you begged us, do you hear? Not one of us, not all of us! We are better without you and we will continue to be, until the end of the world!"

"That's no more than two days away," said Kayn, whose connection to the city's flailing machinery was still keeping him informed.

"Two days is forever," the dying man told him.

Kayn considered it and thought that yes, this was true. There had been no subjective time in the orgynism. Hours had been the same as centuries, and centuries the same as hours. That it lasted as long as it had was therefore the same thing as not lasting for a heartbeat, a crowning achievement the same thing as a total failure. This truism, it further struck him, was also true of the city itself, and, to a still larger extent, the history of all humanity, a race that had been around for many billions of years and had turned out to be as ephemeral as a sneeze. He thought: *How many terribly depressing things are also tremendously freeing?* and embraced that epiphany, feeling much better.

"Enjoy your two days," he told the man functioning as the voice of the orgynism.

"Go to hell."

• • • •

In the past, when great ships sank far from land, those left aboard in the final moments had to choose between two options. One was to stay aboard the vessel for as long as they could, and in so doing embrace what life-preserving properties it still had, at the cost of submitting themselves to the prospect of being dragged with it down into blackness. The other was to damn the dubious comforts of that which would not float for long, dive into the turbulent sea, and swim like mad, knowing that there was no other vessel to swim to, but still embracing fate, challenging the universe to provide deliverance while it still could. There had always been advocates of both methods, people who had lived and died by both methods, people who had doomed themselves by making the wrong choice. The right choice had never been anything but circumstance.

Aware of this, and aware that his own preferred strategy would soon be moot, Kayn trekked through streets that were coming apart even as he traveled on them, to the spot he had chosen for his own egress. His strategy was, as it turned out, not a unique one; there were a dozen others, comprising the largest crowd he had seen in one place since departing his orgynism, in line ahead of him, waiting for their own leap into stormy waters. He watched one or two of them go, and then sat cross-legged on the floor, to do the one thing he'd never really done before, the one that he did not think he would have another chance to do after today.

In short, he composed a poem.

He did not ask the machines to compose a sonnet for him. The last time he'd done that, it had turned out to be the worst sonnet ever written. He had no comprehension of that literary form in particular or of the rules of meter or rhyme, and so his wasn't even a sonnet. It was in truth only a poem at all because that was what he had intended to write and because now, at the end of time, it would have been downright silly for even the most persnickety critic in all the world to make a fuss about definitions. Besides, honestly, it was more than fair to say that Kayn had accomplished the goal sought by all the poets who had written in all of Mankind's languages, since the beginning of time: for their words to last until the end of time. Though Kayn managed this trick by composing his just a few minutes before that grand departure, his seizure of this ancient goal could not be denied. His words, as heartfelt as any that had ever been written, would last to the dying of the light.

He struggled with the most important part, the lines that summarized everything he'd ever learned.

When nothing matters, everything matters.
When everything matters, everything's tragedy.
When everything's tragedy, everything's comedy.
When everything's comedy, nothing matters.

He was sufficiently proud of this to show it to the man standing ahead of him in line, who wore a stained black suit and a matching top hat, all gone ragged and stinking from many years without laundering. That man read the lines, seemed to consider delivering the judgment that it was incomprehensible gibberish, but lit up at that one highlight, saying, "Oh, very good. Very, very good. That summarizes the idiocy of the species more than anything."

"Do you really think so?" asked Kayn, who with this question became the last human being to ever care what a critic thought of his work.

The man in the battered top hat replied in the affirmative and placed himself on the conveyer belt into the orifice, surrendering his eternal fate to whatever it chose to make of him. On the other end lay the things that had been the other people on line: a lampshade, a golden helix, a blinking lizard, a globe, a puff of smoke, a parasol, a gasping fish, a mound of gray sand. Perhaps two or three of these things remained conscious of what it had been before their transformations. Perhaps two or three would survive after the city was gone. There was no way to predict, really. Submitting to the change might or might not be a better survival strategy than finding some secure place and waiting for the city to be engulfed. But this was the choice of those who found themselves on sinking ships: to stay, or to leave, either option equally promising, either option equally bad, the choice ultimately a lesson in philosophy. When that was the only thing left, the only weapon left was confidence.

Kayn was confident. For him, at least, it would not end this way.

In the meantime, he stood by as the penultimate man went through, and awaited his own turn.

SAND CASTLES

They met day-drinking.

It was cold and wet, not quite raining but threatening to, in the way that storms do even when they don't then intend on getting on with it; and though they each might have spent the day in a bar anyway, this one lent itself to being spent indoors and the atmosphere just kind of lent itself to drinking.

It was late morning when they began, the first customers in a small-town corner joint that still smelled of the night before. They were at opposite ends of the bar and what with one thing or another they struck up a conversation. It just became easier to sit together, even though neither one of them had begun the day looking for someone to spend time with. They were both well-versed in the drinker's skill of maintaining the right buzz by neither drinking too much or too little, and it didn't matter to either one of them that the other was less than perfect company for any other occasion, or that they both smoked too much.

His name was Loren. Hers was Lauren. This struck them as disproportionately hilarious and they pointed it out to everybody who came in and sat anywhere near them. It turned out that they'd both been married and divorced, that they both had grown kids they didn't speak with much, and that they'd both lived in town all their lives, except for her two years as a failed college student and his as a fuckup soldier. Their failure to ever meet up with each other before also struck them as disproportionately hilarious, enough that they drank to it, and this too went on for a while until he said,

"I like you."

She said, "You're okay."

"That the best compliment you can give?"

"It's a perfectly fine compliment. You're a funny guy."

"Ha. That's the way I like to be remembered. A funny guy. Like I'm spinning at high speeds and tossing out witticisms like shrapnel." He shook his head. "But there's a bit of an insult hidden behind that compliment, isn't there?"

"Far as I'm concerned, it just means you're a funny guy."

"You ever see that old movie, *Goodfellas?*"

"I don't give a shit about movies."

"Bunch of Mafia guys, carousing in a bar. One calls another a funny guy and for a minute there it looks like he's gonna take serious offense. You wonder if someone's gonna get shot or something."

"All I know is I never heard of it. I just meant you're a funny guy."

He said, "I'll take it, I guess."

"Imagine my relief."

Then he said, "Hey, you ever see the castle?"

"What castle?"

"You know. The one everyone's been talking about. Out by the water."

She made a foggy connection. *That* thing. She remembered people talking about it, some last night in this very room. "Been thinking of a taking a look. Too many things to do."

He said, "It looks like rain. Phil, don't you think it looks like rain?"

The establishment's windows were too tinted to allow easy transparency, delegating all serious assessments of the weather to that category of patron willing to go outside and look up, but Phil the day bartender had long since learned that with a certain other category of patron, reflexive agreement was the easiest route to peace. "Yeah, been that way."

Loren said, "We wait too long, rain's gonna frickin' destroy the thing."

Lauren said, "So?"

"So what is it? Three blocks to the beach? We should take a look while we have a chance."

She examined her drink, which was one quick swallow from extinction. Of course, that failed to consider the drink she could have next, which some part of her already mourned. *And then,* the automatic thought came, *one after that,* and this was a delightful prospect, but part of her remembered those old days when alcohol had been the route to spontaneity, the lubrication that had made her unpredictable, instead of the presence who could be counted on to still be perched on the same stool, two or three hours from now. An unscheduled trip to go see a castle struck her as a fine tribute to her vanished whimsicality. "Yeah, sure."

They left the bar and started heading toward the shore. It was a waterfront town that always smelled of sea breezes, one that always lived by the weather that came rolling in from the water; one that, upon turning cold, really turned cold, which is why the air now wore on their bones like a coat that had been soaked in brine before being donned wet. To the extent that either Loren or Lauren ever noted changes in the weather, they had both noted that the weather had held this way for almost ten days, without ever congealing into rainfall; but yes, Phil had been right. Sure. It did sure as hell look like rain.

They made it to the place where the road dead-ended in a wooden barrier, just before a strip of tall grass separating the inhabited streets from the beach. A few moments spent on the narrow sandy path that cut between pavement and sand, they reached the beach, where gray water lapped against the shore, depositing seaweed and other debris.

Here, on the beach, sat an immense sand castle.

It had been sculpted over the course of three frenzied days by a team of artists who had seen fit to become world-class competitors at that delightful but largely irrelevant skill, who had come to the beach at the tail end of warm weather to create an ephemeral masterwork. Crowds had gathered to watch the construction in delight. There had been newspaper stories, TV news segments, the inevitable YouTube videos, all in service of this local sensation that would melt into a shapeless ruin at the first substantial rain. Almost everybody who lived within walking and driving distance, who had any sense of whimsy or wonder at all, had already come to see it, just to record the site within their own gray matter; then the weather had changed, and the crowds had thinned, abandoning it to its inevitable destruction by the elements.

It was immense, by the standard of such things. It was surrounded by a four-foot wall, sculpted to simulate brickwork. A narrow walkway under a low arch—still intact—simulated the drawbridge over a moat. There was a sign on a stick there, reading, PLEASE KEEP OUT! SCULPTURE IS FRAGILE! Inside, after a courtyard, stood the castle, ten feet high, an intricate structure with towers and ramparts and windows. A portico gate, guarded by two sand-figures standing at either side, was down, barred entrance to the inner structure, but there was enough black space visible through the gaps that it was easy to imagine that the extraordinary level of detail continued inside, complete with throne room, royal quarters, and the inevitable scheming of courtiers. The entrance itself was like an arched mouse-hole, just large enough that if the portico ever lifted, it was also possible to imagine entering the interior on hands and knees.

Lauren hadn't given any thought to what her reaction to this place would be—mild amusement, maybe—but was unprepared for what it actually was: sadness. This castle may have been a whimsical folly, but it was also a monument to somebody's enthusiasm, to the joy they had taken in the effort to produce something that, however short-lived, nevertheless gave pleasure to those who beheld it. She could not help but contrast it to her own daily existence, the alimony that supported her, the part-time job that picked up the slack (and that she was about to lose), the grown children who had lives of their own and who had sworn off letting her into them. This was a place where somebody had shared a form of joy, and it struck her as an affront to her own existence, which had become an exercise in numbing herself. The thought put her in significant danger of getting sloppy.

Loren said, "I'm telling you, somebody needed to get a life."

She realized that he'd brought them here hoping that they would both then laugh at it, and coupled with her last thoughts this made her apathetic acceptance of the man turn into a form of virulent dislike. "Why?"

"I mean, it's impressive and everything, but it's still a stupid waste of effort that's going to melt away after the next storm. Look, I didn't mean anything by it. Want a shot?"

"You carrying?"

He produced a flask with a hearty ta-daa, she joined him in a drink, and the two of them drank to the kingdom of sand. It was the kind of drink that left her feeling thirstier, as so many of them were these days. Sating that thirst was a project far more ephemeral than this project of sand could ever be.

Then he said, "Let's head back."

The inevitable rest of the day stretched out before her before a weather-beaten old melody, one heard too many times to still perceive as music.

"I think I'll stay a while."

"Are you kidding? It's pretty and everything, but I've pretty much sucked all the possible enjoyment out of it."

She said, "I haven't."

His eyebrows furrowed, the way those of a certain subspecies of man do when confronted with something beyond comprehension. It was the precursor to affront, and affront could be the precursor to anything from calling her a bitch and storming off, to erupting into violence. Maybe he'd thought she'd follow him home for a quickie. Maybe he'd choose as secondary option raping and murdering her right now. While those brows remained furrowed, both outcomes seemed equally likely.

She said, "Go back to the bar, if you want. I'll be back in about twenty minutes."

"What are you going to do in the sand for twenty minutes?"

"I just want to, you know, take this in a little longer."

That look of affront again. "Why?"

"Look. I just want to be alone for a bit."

Again, it could have gone either way, and again, she spent that heartbeat waiting to see how he would fall. Then he rolled his eyes, mumbled something to the effect that she could do what she wanted, and left her there. She watched him go, this man with the name like hers, watched him return to the strip of grass separated the beach from the city streets, his gait just a little unsteady, as hers must be, and in that moment it occurred to her that she knew exactly what his life had been, and what it would be, down to the day his cooling body was found on some bare urine-soaked mattress. He had seven years, she knew. Only seven. It was a ridiculous and wholly uncharacteristic moment of clairvoyance, and chances were that it wasn't even close to accurate; hell, if she'd ever been able to tell the future, she likely wouldn't have gotten married, had kids, or allowed herself to be bought her first drink. She would have bought more lottery tickets but wasted less of her money on wrong numbers. It was just a momentary whimsy. But for the moment she had faith in it. Seven years.

She figured she had less, and she didn't care all that much. It had been a while since her own life had been any goddamned fun. Some days, oblivion was the only satisfaction worth having.

Sighing, she turned her attention back to the portcullis, specifically those dark spaces behind the grillwork, and specifically to those black spaces between the vertical and horizontal bars, spaces so black that to her eyes they certified deeper chambers beyond. She squinted to make the best use of the available light and made out a miniature vestibule, ending in a set of double doors an arm's-length away. Even there, where none of the people on the beach could see, the attention to detail was extraordinary. The two sand figures standing guard at both sides of the door were both at attention, but there were tiny differences between them, testimony that they were individuals and not duplicates. She could make out the hinges on either side of the door, even some of the wood grain on the door itself. A thin line of light visible beneath the double doors seemed to shift, testifying to some motion on the other side, and she did not question what kind of creature must have been moving in the chamber beyond: a mouse, a sand crab, even a little knight-errant. She only knew that there had to be one, and just like that, it struck her that she needed to identify it.

She inserted her fingers through the gaps in the grille, and made fists, crumbling that gate into the sand it was made of. An unobstructed view of the double doors, flooded with relative light, provided her with the intelligence that they and the guards at either side were every bit as detailed as they had seemed to be when that view was filtered; even more so. She could make out individual planks in those double doors, now, and yes, from the shifting light under those doors, something was indeed moving behind them, little thin patches of darkness that duplicated the way such light is interrupted whenever it is eclipsed by the passing steps of people. Had she not been a little drunk, and a little sloppy about being drunk, she might have noted the mystery but backed off, thinking that the last thing she wanted to do was interfere with something that was none of her business; but she was drunk and she did not want to return to the bar or (part of her realized) to anything else that awaited her in the direction of her everyday life. And so she squeezed herself into the opening head first, her shoulders scraping the walls and the top of her head scraping the arched ceiling as she pulled herself forward, into the darkness.

The armored guards, who had been standing at attention, spears at the ready, now recoiled. They retreated as far as they could against the end of the vestibule, and why not? From their point of view, the monster before them was a giant, a thing born of magic and animated by worse things, with long clawed fingers digging deep gouges in the stone floor as she dragged herself further down the passage and toward everything they were pledged to protect. Lesser men might have had their minds shattered at the very sight of her. But theirs was not a world of the true middle ages, not if the fanciful extent of the sculpture around them could be believed; theirs was a world where orcs and dragons must surely exist, if only at a remove that required a quest to find them. And so, they did what brave guards in their position would have had to do. They overcame their terror and charged, jabbing their spears into Lauren's knuckles. For their sake, it was just unfortunate that the relative solidity of their fantasy weapons, and her flesh, held. Their spears not only failed to penetrate her skin, but also disintegrated into their component grains at the very attempt, leaving the two brave guards even more terrified, even more awestruck as she ignored their resistance and, with another energetic heave, pulled herself closer to those double doors.

They swung inward, and a horde of little sand-warriors rushed out, screaming the way warriors do, shouting words in some language Lauren didn't know that were clearly orders to die in defense of the king. They swarmed her arms and swarmed her chest and jabbed their little sand-spears into her, or more properly at her, as none penetrated. Some went for her face and this was a problem, their substance getting into her mouth or, more problematic, her eyes, but she flailed her arms and broke legions of the little bastards into their component fragments, until the vestibule she'd invaded was inches-deep in them: a sea of what would have been their viscera, had they possessed viscera and not tightly-packed sand. A few who escaped her reach saw no valor in continuing to fight a behemoth who could not be hurt, and fled back through the double doors, into the chambers beyond, presumably to help the last stand there. Nobody barred those doors, likely because they saw no point. Lauren coughed out a cloud of grit, rammed her clawing fingertips into the tile of the vaster room beyond, and pulled herself onward, breaking through the double doors and collapsing the adjacent walls as she burst through into what turned out to be the magnificent space beyond.

It was the throne room, so vast even at its scale that there was more than enough space for her. It was larger than it physically could have been, given the total dimensions of the sand castle as it existed on the beach; large enough to function as a perfectly respectable living room, on her own scale. The space that in her own life would have had a couple of couches, a low coffee table festooned with aging magazines and junk mail, and the other clutter of her everyday life, was for the little sand-people a cavernous, awe-inspiring cathedral, complete with vaulted ceiling and discrete shafts of light stabbing through the gloom via skylights in the sculpted ceiling. Any petitioner from outside the castle would have been astounded by the vast emptiness before him, the distance between those double doors and the throne, which occupied an elevated stage on the other side of the hall; a space meant to intimidate, to terrify ambassadors from lesser kingdoms and to remind any subject that the seated figure surrounded by warriors was their lord and the lord of all he surveyed. Rising to a crouch once she was fully inside the hall, a short scramble away from the inner powers of the kingdom, Lauren didn't press her advantage. Instead she sat, cross-legged, the sand cold but dry beneath her, and faced that stage.

There were about fifty of them, she supposed, some in armor, some in finery, all gathered close to the king, a bearded figure wearing a crown that the sculptors had adorned with jewels, or at least sand-flecks of different and brighter colors. From a distance they evoked rubies and emeralds set in shining gold, and they gave weight to the little visage of the man beneath, whose precise expression was too small and too far away to read in much detail, but was likely grim. Lauren was fairly impressed that he was not ordering his guards to whisk him away to some place of safety, but instead remained where he sat, waiting to see what the situation required.

"I guess to you I'm like some kind of big scary giant, huh."

The words rumbled and echoed. They reverberated off the high ceiling, bounced off the elaborate tapestries, no doubt carried past this throne room and through the corridors of power behind the throne, to the hidden passages where servants hurried past one another on their various errands, to the barracks of the king's soldiers, to the lesser quarters of the peasants and slaves. However far this place extended—and at the moment she had the impression that it went far beyond anything she could see, to many, many layers of creation she could not even guess at—there could be no place beyond the reach of her voice. Her terrible, thundering voice.

There was no way to tell whether the sand-people understood her or simply interpreted her voice as the roars of an invader who had, for the moment, stopped advancing. Certainly, some of the more cowardly figures at the end of the hall recoiled in their own, individual way; some ducked out through a passage behind the throne, one or two fell to their knees, and a young woman wearing a Renaissance-Faire conical hat with a long strip of some diaphanous material dangling from its tip drew closer to the figure on the throne, seeking strength and perhaps protection from his presence, as if there were really anything he could have done to shield him from any wrath Lauren might have been in any danger of venting. But for now, they waited.

"Yeah, that's me," she said. "A big scary monster." A deep breath, and she continued, "I kind of shut down everything I ever had, you know? My marriage wasn't such hot shit, but I contributed. My kids are wastes of oxygen who don't call me anymore, but I made them that way. I got a bad back and a shitty liver and I knocked down every connection I ever had the way those guys in the Godzilla suits knocked down buildings. It helped that pretty much everybody I ever dealt with was a prick or a bitch of one kind or another, but I don't fool myself: I contributed. I'm just not stupid enough to think I can do something about it, at this stage. So, I don't know. Maybe I'll be *your* monster. I dunno. Maybe I'll be some good at that."

This caused some furtive murmuring among the courtiers of sand.

Lauren licked her lips. She had never carried a flask because it had been years since she'd allowed herself to be any fair distance from her next drink, but right now, with sand in her hair and in her throat and the air around her so stale and so warm compared to the relative chill of the beach, she would have liked a snort, something to bolster her until she decided what to do next.

Then something happened on the king's side of the hall. Two of the armored guards left the stage, carrying a struggling young woman between them. She was not the princess in the conical hat, but some kitchen maid or something like that, based on the apron she wore. Her size again made it impossible to make out any facial expression, but her wild thrashing testified to outright panic, and her tiny head kept forming a dimple where her mouth would have been, in exactly the shape screams would have made. With little effort at all they dragged her to the center of the hall, the midway point between the throne and Lauren herself, and there they forced her to her knees, before one drew a sword and slit her open from neck to navel. Sand-bowels spilled out upon the sand-tile, and the two soldiers bowed before backing off and returning to the royals on their elevated stage.

"What the hell was that?"

She crawled toward the pathetic little corpse and probed it with her fingertip. It naturally collapsed into its component grains at first touch, neither as wet nor as steaming with the processes of life that it had seemed to be until that moment. It had been one hell of a pantomime, one astonishing puppet-show about a young woman being offered up as sacrifice by her craven king, but that was all it had been. It was just part of the same trick, magic or whatever else you wanted to call it, that moved them all, once sculpted; not life, but something that imitated life.

Lauren spread the sand the little figure had been in a circle, patting it down hard until it became part of the same simulated stone floor it lay on, and then she faced the huddled figures by the throne, and she found herself hating them as much as she'd hated anything on this poor, dying Earth.

"Yeah, well, I don't accept your goddamned offering, what do you think of that?"

The only response to that was a sudden, painful jab in her calf.

"Ow, what the f—"

Another jab, not at the same spot but right next to it, doubled her agony. She recoiled and reached for the source of the pain and felt a fresh strike, this time on her palm, which in an instant felt on fire. She glanced down and saw blood pulsing from a slice in her palm, before the source of her pain struck yet again, this time providing her with a clear look at the weaponry used against her.

Two sand-warriors held a shard of broken glass.

It had to have been some piece of broken bottle, maybe some ancient coke bottle, maybe some more recent vessel for booze, shattered and abandoned on either the beach or that forlorn strip of grass between the beach and the civilized streets beyond; the kind of thing that lay in wait for some hapless beach-comber, walking the sand in bare feet. Every beach that has ever known the tread of a human foot has also harbored such hidden hazards, and years after the overall migration to plastic bottles still did, some no doubt buried far beneath the sand, some just waiting for the right foot to land in the wrong way.

To these sand-people, watching as the impervious leviathan cried out in agony at its touch, it had to be the equivalent of one of those fantasy swords from the movies Lauren had sometimes been too apathetic to turn off, the only thing capable of saving their little kingdom at this hour of its greatest need.

Even as she watched, the two warriors bearing the shard too heavy or too solid for just one of them gathered their courage and charged her leg again, the bloody edge of their weapon foremost.

She didn't carefully formulate a defense. She just lashed out. She brought her fist down, screeching as the glass cut deep into the side of her hand, but mashing the two bearers flat. The two of them exploded in a cloud of sand. One was reduced into a mound, only recognizable as the remains of a sand figure because of the one twitching leg that somehow remained intact; the other was only crushed from the waist down and was left staring at the debris his lower half had become, his mouth contorting in a silent scream. Her own scream matched his because she'd managed this victory only at further cost to her hand, and with absolute fury that she pulled the shard from her fist and threw it to one side, imbedding it in a sandy tapestry too high up the wall for the little people to reach.

"Even here," she said.

She was not thinking clearly enough to put her complaint into complete sentences, but if pressed she might have said that in a world that had done all it could to wound her, even this one showed its willingness to draw blood.

She wanted to charge the throne and all the little people gathered around it, and to pound them into the nothingness they had come from, but her hand and her leg throbbed and the last thing she needed was to get the wounds dirtier, more filled with the stuff of these creatures of silicate. Instead she'd just leave. But none of this crawling across the dirt to get through a narrow tunnel, not anymore; not when everything in sight crumbled at her slightest touch. Not when these little bastards weren't even real.

She'd just tear the walls down, like Samson.

She rose to almost her full height, having to stoop only a little bit beneath that arched ceiling, and it really was satisfying the way the little things cowered and cringed at the sight, at the way she scraped a ceiling so high above their heads that they must have seen it as a tribute to their little kingdom's majesty, and because it seemed the thing to do, she roared, actually roared, putting her full throat into it, taking pleasure in how terrible she was, how wonderful it was to be in a world she could break instead of the one that had broken her. She drew back her fist and drove her whole arm through that arch of sand, hitting open air, before pulling armfuls of the sculpted roof back down into the chamber. To little things their size, it must have been like seeing the end of their world, this destruction of the keep where their king had ruled above all. To Lauren, it was like breaking out of a cage, admitting the air and the light, opening up this space so much like a grave to a sky that, even if gray with clouds, was still bright enough to imply the presence of a sun. The sand began to pile around her ankles, the walls far too crumbly to climb, but as she began pulling them down, obliterating the tapestries, returning the false castle to its origins of sand; the destruction she made gave her fresh earth to stand on, and this she climbed, pulling herself out, no longer interested in the false terror of the false creatures of the false court below.

She pulled herself back in open air, where legions of archers arrayed on the towers and ramparts loosed their shafts. Little needles of sand struck her shoulders and chest, like all the rest of their weapons except for that shard of glass disintegrating on impact, barely making an impression. Still, she roared at them, a kraken taking pleasure in their puny defiance, toppling one of the intact towers with one mighty blow. Its collapse brought down one of the walkways, dropping dozens of the bastards into the ruin below. She pressed her knee against the growing sandpile supporting her escape and pulled herself upward, until she knelt atop the mostly shattered castle, bloody and irritated and taking a breather while the remaining defenders—and really, there seemed no end to them— fired more volleys of useless arrows, no more dangerous to someone of her scale and solidity than grit carried by errant breeze.

Still, she couldn't afford to stay here and continue battling them, even if they had no more shards in their armory; the last thing she wanted was for anybody from town to happen by and see her destroying this grand castle, in what they would have to interpret as a drunken rampage. Her reputation was not great, but that was something she'd never live down. She might even be prosecuted.

And so, she slid down a collapsing wall back to the courtyard that separated the outer wall from the castle proper, riding an avalanche of sand as it engulfed little panicking sand-people attempting and failing to flee this horrible cataclysm. When she reached the bottom, rising on wobbly legs and blinking from the sand that was now in her hair, in her clothes, and caked on her eyelashes, a few of the sand-people still remained between her and the wall, trapped by the very architecture that she could imagine them once trusting to provide safety; and a few of them had drawn swords and stood before a mob of trembling common- ers and the even smaller figures of children, brandishing the weapons they must have now surely known would not slow her down even by the duration of a heartbeat.

Lauren considered obliterating them and those they were giving their all to protect, but the prospect made her tired and weepy.

"I'm sorry. It's just, you know. Par for the course. I wreck everything."

She sniffed, turned her back, brushed the debris from hair that by now must have resembled a rat's nest, slapped the clouds of sand from her upper clothing, and headed back toward the gap in the fortress wall.

She had no plans except to get home somehow, to strip off these clothes, to shower until she felt clean again, and to go on with her life.

She stopped when she saw what lay in wait for her.

She had come from a beach where the sand looked the way sands do, on beaches traversed by human beings: rippled by winds and by the impact of human steps. Beyond that there had been the ocean in one direction, that grass barrier and her town in another. There had been buildings, the sounds of traffic, a sign to the effect that no lifeguard was on duty off-season and that all bathers entered the water at their own risk. Here and there, litter. She specifically remembered an abandoned, filthy pool noodle tipped with flecks of salt, a broken beach lounge, and at the high-tide mark beyond which the sand was a gentle slope worn smooth by recent waves, the usual demarcation line of deposited seaweed.

None of this was what she saw now.

No, in place of the world she had seen with her male namesake Loren was a sandy kingdom stretching from here to the horizon. She saw a tiny sand village, of sand thatched huts and a little sand windmill, by a stream fed by distant, snow-capped sand-mountains. She saw another sand-fortress, the same scale as this one, occupying the nearest of a series of sandy hills just before a sand-forest. She saw a sky no longer slate-gray but dirt-brown, hiding a sun she was grateful not to see, because it now seemed likely that it would be the same color, and this would have been the blow to shatter what composure still remained, now that she was beginning to understand the kind of place where she now found herself, the kind of fate to which she'd condemned herself.

It was from this vantage point that she heard the distant rumble.

It was the first sound, except for the little puffs of dissolving sand, that she'd heard anybody make in this place. It was rhythmic in its way, too chaotic to resolve into anything as organized as a single identifiable beat.

Then a ragged black line emerged over that nearest hilltop.

Someone, either allied kingdoms or distant outposts of this one, had dispatched cavalry to take on the rampaging monster. They swallowed up the landscape with the speed of their charge, chittering and squealing as they came, and there were more of them than she could bring herself to believe.

There weren't thousands.

That would have been crazy, not that anything about this wasn't crazy.

The hundreds that were coming would be enough, given what they rode.

It took them less time to close the distance than she ever would have expected, given that they had so far to ride; or maybe it just looked far, given the differences in scale between the world she knew and this one where Lauren found herself. They brandished pikes and swords and axes of harmless sand, that could not possibly harm her, but they brought with them something far more dangerous. Just as the little people in this castle had appropriated a shard of glass for their most powerful weapon, so had these distant allies brought along something else that could reasonably be encountered on the beach or on the strip of grass separating it from the town beyond; or even, were they motivated to travel farther in search of resources, in that town itself.

They rode rats, and the sand formed clouds in their wake.

The first wave leaped at her, scratching and clawing at her legs, racing up her body to get at the more vulnerable places higher up. Lauren screamed and kicked, sending some of the little bastards flying, crushing others beneath her heel, but their legs were many and their claws were sharp and they were too many to outfight. She seized one that had reached her thigh—crushing its rider even she as grasped the squirmy thing's neck—and flung it as far as she could, but there were more leaping at her, ever more, and if she stayed here it would be no time at all before they flayed her to the bone. The shattered sand fortress blocked the way behind her, but there was nothing but open space in front of her, and she leaped over the bulk of the army, hitting the sand hard and running as fast as her ravaged legs could carry her. Even as she ran, the rats who had already grabbed hold still sought to bring her down, and she shrieked like a woman in flames as she gave some of her attention to punching them, ripping them free, kicking them where they fell, stumbling, scrambling back to her feet and running still more, the sound of thundering pursuit never far behind.

She ran a straight line for as long as she could stand it. She did not go out of her way to trample any sand-people she encountered along the way, but neither did she make any special effort to avoid their villages, their isolated farmhouses, or the occasional wandering individual who she came across while putting whatever distance she could between herself and the pursuing cavalry of sand and rats. She tore what would have been a bloody swath through the realm, had it only been a realm of flesh and bone; instead, the only blood upon the sand was hers, from a dozen places where glass or teeth had ripped holes in her. It was wholesale destruction, if nothing else, and it left a path of ruin that, if these people had stories, or songs, or histories that they passed from one generation to the next, would be remembered by their descendants as one of their most epic legends, the time the riders drove off the giant thing who had come to lay waste to everything that existed.

Lauren was not a long-distance runner—was, indeed, soon winded from too many years of drink and indolence and smoking—and it was not long before her flight became a gasping lurch. Even then, there were still pursuers behind her, their numbers reinforced by riders from other villages and castles encountered on the way. They didn't press the assault, seeing no reason in throwing good lives after bad, but they did stay close, the rats chittering and the riders brandishing fresh shards of broken glass, to keep her going. Aware that if she fell to her knees, her pursuers would seize the opportunity to finish her off, she kept going, and going, toward those mountains.

She stumbled into what she perceived as a shallow ditch and which by the scale of these sand-people was probably a respectable valley, finding herself thigh-deep deep in flowing water. This was deep enough for her passage to overturn a crowded three-story riverboat traveling downstream that was unlucky enough to be within range of the tsunami caused by her passage. She had no idea how anything made by the people of this civilization managed to survive water at all, and was at this point too intent on her own problems to reflect that this was the very nature of technology, the creation of things that could survive environments the people could not. She did see a couple of dozen little sand-people lined up along the ship's railing recoiling as she thrashed closer, and the way the water she'd churned up inundated the deck, literally washing them away where they stood. The ship rocked in the turbulence, then capsized. Hundreds tumbled into the water, some of them popping to the surface just long enough for their mouths to contort into silent screams, before they vanished in little puffs of cloudy water. Forced into retreat as she'd been, she could not deny taking a certain savage pleasure in still being able to cause mass death and destruction on their scale, a satisfaction she continued to feel as she rose out of the water to find a busy little riverfront town with markets and inns and even one structure she would have bet money was a brothel, all of which she ripped gouges from before pressing on, toward those mountains. She had no choice. The sand-people could not swim, but their cavalry could, and there they were, crossing the water in a glistening brown carpet, unbothered by the current.

Still she ran, or more accurately stumbled, weeping and wondering why she even bothered. The mountains grew nearer. She was maybe what in her world would have been the equivalent of a long city block away when she made up her mind that they were not more sand-sculptures, but clusters of boulder, rising a couple of hundred feet above the sand. For Lauren, they were steep hills. For the sand-people, they must have been what she'd first called them, mountains. But they were stone. They were solid. They would support her. She would not drive herself to exhaustion, fighting earth that shifted beneath her every step, that sent her sliding one foot back for every two she advanced. She would be able to climb, put distance between herself and that army, maybe even find a place where they would not go, where she could stop and think about long-term survival.

And once she got to the base of the rocks, this is what she did, gasping and collapsing and weeping and pulling herself upward and finding the strength to continue even as her wounded legs left stains to mark her passage. About twenty paces up, she stumbled, landed on her knee, felt a fresh eruption of agony, and howled. It was a shriek she would have claimed louder than anything that had ever come out of her mouth, but this would have been a lie; before her marriage broke up, she and her piece of crap husband had screamed at one another in exactly that tone of voice, with exactly the same level of rage and despair. But this was the loudest scream she'd ever uttered without any words, the closest she'd ever come to an animalistic roar. That roar said, *come any closer and I'll kill you!*

When she finally calmed enough, she looked down to the base of the mountain and saw the army that had driven her here, cheering.

She could not hear their cheers. Their little mouths still made no sound her ears could hear. But the body language was unmistakable. There they were, in their hundreds, being joined by others from allied castles, who had sought the glory of the fight. They waved their little sand swords and their little sand axes and their little sand pikes, and they cried their defiance of the unstoppable monster they had forced to flee. A few were even mooning her. They didn't follow her up into the heights, though there was no reason to suppose they couldn't. Those rats would have carried them. But she was away from their lands now, a spent threat no longer worth worrying about. They would not bother themselves with bloodying her any further, not when there were celebrations to be had.

She considered descending into their midst and taking as many with her as she could.

But she was self-destructive, not suicidal.

And so she did the only thing she could.

She went back to climbing.

* * * *

This is what she found. This is how she lived.

Near the peak she found a little alcove where one fallen stone had come to rest beside another. It was a respectable cave, out of the sun and—since it turned out that the temperatures around here could be very cold at night—out of the elements as well. It was just big enough to provide shelter, and though she tried a number of other places, on the other side of the rocks—though she ventured far enough into the desert on the other side to confirm that there were no creatures of sand there—it ended up being the most congenial place for her to live, if this was where she had to live. It was, and so she did. She found another shallow stream not far away, where there were fish; along its banks a few scraggly bushes with berries that fermented easier than she dared to believe, a few things like sticks and stones she could use to make tools.

Although at least part of every day had to be spent keeping herself watered and fed. Unless she had to, she never ventured to the inhabited side of her little mountain. She sometimes spent hours on what she came to call the safe side of the mountain. But when the sun grew low in the dun sky, she returned to her little cave, nibbled on fish and berries and moss and the occasional wandering rat, comforted herself with what intoxication she could manage from the juice of those berries, and contemplated a sky filled with unfamiliar constellations.

For a while she used the edge of a flat stone to mark a nearby wall with hash-marks to commemorate the passage of time, but she kept that up for only a few months before abandoning the project as pointless. By then it was clear that her clothing would be rotting off her. She abandoned it willingly. Her wounds became scars. Her hair grew long and matted. She gained callouses on the soles of her feet and on the palms of her hands. She stopped walking upright and surrendered to the gait that scrambling up and down these rocks rewarded, using all fours. Eventually it became easier to practice the same on her daily trips down to the water. She fell out of the habit of talking, but sometimes, when the berries produced a batch finer than average, sang. At such times, though she had no way of knowing this, the wind carried the sound down from her mountain home, and across the land repairing itself from her rampage, and in this way told those who lived there that the behemoth of legend still lived, up there in the cursed rocks where no one ever went. And in this way, she lived, and in this way she would eventually die, and though she wailed sometimes, it must be said that the life suited her, and that at times she was, if not precisely happy, then at least content.

This is what she found. This is how she lived, and it should be no surprise that this is how she died.

And if this seems to you that her existence had come to nothing, this is something else you should know.

From time to time, down in the realm where the men and women of sand built their homes and fought their wars and pursued the politics of their kind, there once in a while rose those not satisfied with the way things were, those who thought that the fates had greater destinies in mind for them.

Men and women, they would turn their eyes toward the mountains the wise warned against, the place that marked the end of the civilized world. They would remember the stories of the creature who had appeared out of nowhere and wreaked great destruction before being driven back to that place, where it was assumed it belonged, the place that still emanated strange sounds only the leviathan could have made. It would occur to these restless ones that the monster was a sight worth seeing, a quest worth pursuing; a thing worth slaying, for the menace it had once been, and the one it might become again. And so, defying the advice of their families, of their learned, of all those who made lists of the stupid ways the restless before them had gotten themselves killed, they would arm themselves with the finest weaponry they could scavenge, clad themselves in the most impenetrable armor they could find, and they would aim themselves at those mountains, intent on the cave where the monster was said to rest.

Some would stumble on their way up, come to their senses, and return home, saying that they'd searched and searched but could not find any trace of the monster, anywhere.

Others would get as far as their first sight of her, and would either go mad at the very scale of the beast or, again, come to their senses, and head back down. A few would secrete themselves near the place where she laid her head and wait until they saw her sleeping, at which point a number of those would receive the epiphany that as strange as she was, she was at heart just a living thing like any other. It would occur to them that to remove the last of her from the world would be a sin, and then they too would retreat, returning to their world with similar assurances that they had done everything they could but that the beast remained elusive, and might in fact not even exist.

And sometimes, there were the bravest of the brave, those for whom the battle was everything, the ones who bided their time at her cave's mouth, waited for their moment, and then drew their swords or—if they were equipped—their shards of glass, intent on accomplishing what entire legions before them had not. There were, over the years, many of these, all well-meaning. They were heroes and they were fools, two words that often mean the same thing.

Of them, we must report that the little alcove where the monster slept began its life as her home a hard stone surface, no more congenial a bed than concrete would have been, and that over the years it acquired a new and much more comfortable layer, deep enough to render that place as restful a home as the beast could ever want.

BL⊕⊕D REL⊿TIONS

Lise and Mo had been on the road for two days, and were driving through one of the places that drought had turned to drifting sands, when they saw her trudging along the side of the road, the only visible living creature in what was otherwise an expanse of desert between impoverished towns.

The old woman struck Lise as a tough little thing. She wore faded blue jeans and a battered denim jacket. Her silvery gray bun had started to come loose, freeing loose strands to whip behind her in the breeze. She dragged a wheeled suitcase held together with duct tape, and though her gait was determined, there was a significant difference between the distance covered by each tread of her left foot, and the smaller steps managed by the right, rendering her progress lopsided at best. There was no telling how far she'd come, but out here, miles from any relief from the sun, the writing was on the wall for a person of any age, traveling on foot. She might have made another twenty miles, or she might have fallen to her arthritic knees in another hundred yards, but either way, she was in trouble right now, and so Lise could not let the situation be. "Let's stop for her."

Mo said, "She could be anybody."

Between them, Mo had suffered more betrayal at the hands of strangers.

But Lise was the one behind the wheel, and so she said, "That little old thing couldn't break a twig," pulling over when she was three car lengths past the walking woman. Checking the rear-view mirror, she saw that the tiny figure had stopped in mid-step, not panicking, but not hurrying to approach either. She was doing what only made sense, waiting to see what the occupants of the car intended.

Lise got out and walked halfway back to her, her hands in plain sight. She was a classical blonde beauty with large blue eyes and big white teeth, whose smile had for most of her life made people want to smile back. That those returning smiles were sometimes camouflage for predatory intent was not her fault; she began every exchange without any intended malice. "Morning," she said.

"Morning."

The woman dragging the roller case was not as ancient as she'd seemed from behind. She was not some crone about to stumble into her grave. She was a worn but energetic sixty, with permanent lines on her forehead and at the corners of her eyes and at the edges of her lips, and loose strands of silvery hair abandoned by her bun trembled alongside her cheeks, but as small and as wiry as she was, she looked stronger than her limp suggested. Not old, not in the decrepit sense the word often implied. But older, certainly. More than thirty years older than Lise, maybe twenty older than Mo. It was hard to not feel protective.

Lise said, "Can you use a ride?"

"I can. But just so you know, I've been on the road for hours and don't smell too good."

"We have wet wipes. And the windows roll down. Only car rule is no smoking."

"Honey," the older woman said, "I quit tobacco when you were still a gleam in your daddy's eye."

Lise hated that expression. "My Daddy's eye never gleamed."

"The point is, I prefer weed, but I won't pollute your space with it when you're driving."

"We won't make you share. Hop in. I'm Lise."

"Greta. We go any distance, I'll chip in for charging stations."

Greta's hand was rough and calloused, cold to the touch in the way that old hands could be, but her cheeks crinkled with nested smile-lines; the look of someone who would have reminded Lise of some beloved grandmother, had she ever known one. There was no pretense in it, nothing but trust, an almost unheard-of commodity since the fall of the first version of America, that was just beginning to come back in style after the fall of the second.

The woman was not totally careless. She refused an offer to stick her bag in the trunk, and instead kept it with her as she settled into the back seat. The car was a small one, with precious little leg room for anyone not in the front; and there was already one suitcase and a twelve-pack of bottled water back there, making the accommodations tight. Still, Greta slipped into what room there was, right behind the driver's seat, like a spare part fitting in a recess built for her.

By then Mo was turned around in the front passenger seat, one eyebrow raised in that way she had, the kind that said, *I don't know what shit you're packing, but I'm not buying any of it.* She was an older, tougher, butcher, darker, taller, harder-looking woman than Lise – had spent some time in the army, before the late unlamented True America expelled dykes from military service – and she knew how to express pre-emptive warning with a glare, a skill that came in handy even if it was excessive against an old lady whose twig-breaking capacity had already been placed in question.

Lise said, "Mo, this is Greta. Greta, this is Mo."

Greta said, "Thanks. That short for Maureen or Monique?"

"It's the accurate length for Mo. Call me that and don't get on my ass about it. Where you headed?"

"I'm going to the Dedication," Greta said.

"Oh," said Mo, and just like that, it was okay.

· · · ·

The Dedication was two days off and a day-and-a-half drive away. It was certainly farther than a woman with a limp could travel on foot, but as Greta explained, the choice hadn't been up to her. Her junker, held together with spit and good intentions, had died on the side of the road, and because it was such a piece of trash she'd given it up for lost. and started hoofing.

Lise felt a little twinge of affection for her own vehicle, a warhorse almost as old as she was, that bore more than its share of dings and scrapes and made complaining noises every once in a while. It would never be mistaken for the chariot of a couple with money, but at the bare minimum it still moved, and had been a life-saver on a couple of occasions when she and Mo had needed to get out of one town, or another, in a hurry. She said, "You must really want to get there."

"Don't you?"

"But your car."

"It was a piece of crap. All I had, but still, just a thing. I'm not too concerned about things. Not when I've had to let go of people, both ways."

"Both ways?"

"You know. The dead, and the dead to me."

It was not an uncommon way to characterize the people in one's life, in this era after the country's emergence from the hell of True America. "Lots of overlap between those two groups, nowadays," Lise noted.

"Yup."

"In particular, lots of dead I'm not particularly sorry about."

"I'm sorry about all of them," Greta said. "Lots of blood on the ground."

Mo said, "Always has been, Miss Daisy There never was any fucking golden age for this country. You always had to be well-off and white to even think so. For everybody else, it's always been a grindhouse cinema version of *Lord of the Flies*."

Declarations like that were one of Mo's ways of determining whether a new person was even worth engaging with, and Lise was glad to see Greta clear that first hurdle with a simple, "I know."

"Still," Lise said, "You have a point about writing people off. There were lots of people we thought we trusted, before the Truers took over."

"Yup," Greta said again. "But it's always been like that. You only know what people are capable of when you give them the power to do anything they want. I had neighbors turn in neighbors, nice woken people changing direction when they saw what way the wind was blowing. A couple who got ugly to me during the bad times tracked me down when times turned back, to say they hoped I knew that they were never *really* like that. If I'd ever had any use for guns, I would have chased them off my property with both barrels blazing. Instead I just drove them off with words. But they were friends; we broke bread more than once. I never want to see them again, but I still miss them from the days before. You know?"

Mo said, "We know. We both buried our share, breathing or not."

They drove in silence for a while, as the land outside changed character, turned a little greener. They passed through a small town of empty storefronts and decaying homes, some of which still bore the now-tattered flags of True America and in a couple of those there were people in their yards and on their porches, glaring at the strangers passing through. Lise, who was still driving, wrestled with the classical dilemma of outsiders passing through such areas, which is to say whether to pick up speed and leave quickly, or to take her time and therefore avoid the impression of vulnerability that encouraged predators to give chase. She erred on the side of taking her time, to avoid pissing off any malignant local law enforcement. And nobody came after them; before long they were back on the roads outside of town, driving past dying farmland.

• • • •

Mo selected a playlist from the car's database, a feature better maintained than they kept the air conditioning. The first song was somebody they knew from back home, a young woman with a killer voice who delivered her songs as soft confidences, rather than as exercises in reaching high notes; she had once belted for the back row, but had come out of the re-alignment camps singing in this style exclusively, either because she couldn't reach those heights anymore or because everything she'd seen and lived had led to her no longer wanting to. Still, there was love in it, and joy, and the sheer defiance expressed by still being able to sing at all, and for about half an hour the three of them listened to the music of someone who, like them, had made it through the flames, until the first song repeated and Lise switched it off, rather than have the whole set cycle through again.

At length, just to jump-start things, Lise said, "So. Who are you, when you're not on foot in the middle of nowhere?"

"You first," Greta said. "I've been trying to figure out. Am I riding with two friends or a couple?"

"Would that make a difference?"

"Of course not, cuddlebug. I'm just a girl who likes to know who she's riding with."

"We're together," Lise said. "Hope to marry if the new Court brings it back. But now that's a fight we have to have all over again."

"Even if it goes state by state," Mo said. "This trip aside, there's lots of places I'm going to avoid the rest of my life, no matter how much they say they've reformed. Don't want to look at people and wonder what they did, when the shits were in charge."

Greta clucked. "Me too."

"So getting back to you," Lise pressed on, "where's home?"

"Well, as it happens, I already told you. I left it on the side of the road."

There was a moment of respectful, awed silence as much that hadn't made sense about their passenger suddenly resolved into clarity.

"Damn," Mo said.

"We're so sorry," Lise said, simultaneously.

"I'm not. It wasn't about not being able to afford a place. Even in the bad times I was always able to put together enough of that to get by. And the Truers did have their workhouses. But last few years, it was about being able to hit the road at a moment's notice. Lots of reasons why I might have had to run for the border with everything I had."

"And before that?"

Greta let the thought hang for a bit and then said, "Well, I was no one special, really. Married with a couple of kids. Ran a little gift shop in a hotel. They rented me the space and I made it work, helping my man Dan keep food on the table for our boys. We were comfortable. I hate to say, complacent. Then the regime looked into our politics, got Dan fired from his teaching job, and got the hotel to shut me down. He started waxing floors and I started cleaning homes. Not long after that I lost him and my younger, Harleyville."

"I'm so sorry," Lise repeated, aware that she was repeating herself. "Which one was that?"

"The Taiwan Moon."

"Sounds like a Chinese Restaurant."

"It was. Though I wouldn't blame you if you can't summon the story. It happened when there was a fresh incident every few days."

"I remember," Lise said, even though she couldn't be sure of that. There had been so many; theatres, stadiums, schools, anyplace accessible by a malcontent with a gun. killer with a gun. About all they had in common was the aftermath, the victims reported as "passed away" because it was illegal and dangerous to utter the specific, that they'd been shot.

Greta was silent for a while, and for a few seconds Lise was afraid that she'd break into tears or dissolve into hysterics or any of those things that people expect of the grieving, even when like Lise they were grieving themselves and are long past the easy histrionics. But when the little woman spoke again, her voice was calm.

"His name was Freddie and he was seven. I was in the bathroom. I heard the shots, and the screams, but I didn't see it happen. Our food hadn't come yet, and I was just in there washing my hands, so I didn't see it happen. Freddie and Dan, both gone waiting for their curry chicken." "Me, with a shattered knee from a round that made it through the wall. My other boy, Lars, who was ten, he was in the other bathroom, so he lived too. Though he's been dead to me since he was eighteen."

Greta said, "What did he do?"

"He got in trouble, smuggling meds, and they were going to send him to be re-educated. Bought his way out by admitting--I put that word in quotes, 'admitting,'—that his brother never existed. Stood up in front of the Judge and testified that he was an only child and that I'd spent his whole life trying to brainwash him into believing he had a father and brother, that I was just some old subversive who made it up, in order to attack the Second Amendment." She took a deep breath. "Last time I saw him it was at my own trial, when he pointed at me and said, 'You only had one son.' I said, 'Then I have none.' For just a second there I saw him falter, but then the prosecutor called that an admission of guilt, and I was done. I was on the bus to one of the camps an hour later."

"He might still be alive. Not all of them got killed during the reckoning."

"He *is* alive," Greta said. "He has a wife and two kids now, and not long ago he invited me to come visit. I accepted. But while I was there, I made the mistake of mentioning Freddie. And then one of my grand-children said what their daddy had been teaching them all along. *'But Freddie was made up, wasn't he?'* And Lars was dead to me all over again. I just wouldn't tolerate one son erasing the other. Ever."

Greta had said all of this without any undue emotion, except with a slight quiver during the final *ever*. But the words hung in the air anyway, and for a minute Lise was loath to disturb the silence.

Then Lise said, "A long time ago, my father told me that there could be no such thing as an ex-Nazi. The only thing he ever said that I ever agreed with. Goes for Truers too, I guess."

"I don't believe that, cuddlebug. Any number of people buy into toxic madness and then wake up, the way people do from fever. If they didn't, the country wouldn't have even started to try to find its way back. I believe in redemption, very much. But I also believe that it isn't a tro-phy you get just for spinning like a weathervane, to follow changes in the wind. What I learned about Lars on that visit was that he'd do it all again tomorrow, the second another set of True Americans take power. I won't sit with him on birthdays and holidays and pretend I can't see it. I can't. And that's why I'm on this trip, for the one son I can still tell myself wouldn't have been like that."

Another spell of silence, and then Mo said:

"I am so sorry, old woman, but what else did you expect, giving the boy a white-ass name like Lars?"

Lise cried, "Mo!"

But Greta just laughed, and said, "I know, I know. I don't know what I was thinking."

"Lars," Mo repeated, letting the S linger in a hiss. "Shit, it was like you were just *asking* for trouble."

More horror from Lise. "*Damn it, Mo!*"

"Could have been worse," Greta said, adding the words that almost sent them off the road: "I almost named the silly son of a bitch *Chad*."

* * * *

With Greta's story out in the open, Mo and Lise had to quickly go over their own. Quickly meant that they gave totals, not details. Lise said she'd lost a daughter and left it at that. Mo said she'd lost, in her own words, *a whole damn bunch.* By mutual consent the stories were placed on hold. Conversation turned to lighter topics, like the way things used to be, the logistics of the journey, whatever tomfoolery bedeviled a new regime that was easy to complain about only because it was not moving fast enough in reversing the crimes of the last one.

They drove through lunch, subsisting on bottled water, rice cakes and protein bars, with only brief stops at charging stations to top off the car and run in to relieve their anguished bladders. But by the time the afternoon light started to fail they were all ready for a leisurely meal and sanity break, and for a good night's sleep. They found a diner that was open and served better food than any of the three would have believed, though it was expensive as almost all food was nowadays, and half the items on the menu were unavailable due to the crop shortages.

It was dinner time and the place only had about half a dozen customers. They ate their food and found it filling and even splurged on a pecan pie, a delicacy now as extravagant as lobster. The emptiness of the place provided license to sit around and shoot the shit, but eventually they got the impression that they were keeping the waitstaff from going home, and relented.

Signaled, the elderly waitress came over with the check and said, "So, where you ladies headed?"

"Family reunion," Greta said, and this was wholly satisfactory in that it happened to be true.

After that, they got directions to lodging cheap enough to afford but clean enough that it wouldn't leave the three of them itching from bedbugs the next morning. It was a roadside motel in the grand Norman Bates tradition, an inevitable joke that none of the three allowed to go unspoken, and which was rung again in multiple variations during the check-in process. Greta said that she would be comfortable enough sleeping in the car, as long as they let her in to use the shower the next morning, but neither of the other two would have that and so they overcame her objections and got a pair of attached rooms, leaving the connecting doors open. What with one thing or another the three of them spent the rest of that evening in the half of their shared accommodations that they'd originally intended only for Lise and Mo, those two sharing one queen-sized bed while Greta got stoned on the other.

As per their frequent and irritating but also deeply cherished domestic arrangement, Lise made a game go at getting further into her novel while Mo bitched long and hard about whatever happened to be playing on cable. It was, of course, impossible to ignore Mo while she was being hilarious, let alone to advance more than two pages in even the lightest reading, a frequent complaint. At home Mo most often eventually relented out of pity, but here she had a fresh audience member, giggly from weed, who hadn't heard all her favorite routines.

"Would you look at this shit?" Mo hollered at th TV. "Would you just *please* look at this brain-dead shit?"

Greta coughed out smoke. "Is she always like this?"

"Yup," Lise said, irritated in the way that only those we love most can irritate us. "Mo isn't into any narrative that can't be complained about. She doesn't want anything good, she just wants to entertain herself being indignant. And keep me from getting any further into my book."

On the screen, the super-spy's muscle car vaulted from one rooftop to another, somehow bridging the difference even though the two buildings were of identical height and at least fifty feet apart. A helicopter carrying bad guys of indeterminate motivation flew circles around this activity, firing grenades. Buildings blew up, a female lead in a suspiciously clean white tank-top leaped from one collapsing surface to another, and the dialogue eagerly devolved to declarative sentences of four words or less. It was the kind of thing Lise never would have chosen to see of her own volition – she liked movies that made at least some stab at being taken seriously, thought shit like this was part of the murderous syndrome that had summoned True America – but that was precisely the thing that made Mo even more contemptuous, the pretense that anything profound about life could possibly be contained in a two-hour chunk of time, occupied by pretty faces paid to pretend to be people they were not. Mo had more respect for bullshit, and only because it could be called out as bullshit.

"Physics don't work that way!" Mo yelled. "Cars don't work that way! The human body doesn't work that way! Fucking *rooftops* don't work that way!"

One of the thugs hunting the good guys stepped into a fusillade of bullets and courtesy of the sfx budget came apart like a baggie filled with blood.

Mo shut it down with a savage jab of the remote. "Well, *that* part was depressingly accurate."

Greta silently offered her a fresh joint. Mo accepted, and for the next couple of minutes the two of them added to the general murk, while Lise slipped a bookmark into her novel and sat with them, neither partaking nor interrupting, just waiting.

Then Greta said, "So where did you serve?"

Mo rolled her eyes. "Do we have to talk about it?"

"No."

"Then why did you ask?"

"Because I had my turn in the barrel hours ago. And we're still getting to know each other."

"A'ight." Mo took a long drag, held it until her eyes crossed, then spoke with a rasp. "Truth is, they sent me just about every-damn-where. Venezuela for a little bit, before that went up. Then both the big sandbox *and* the big ice, if you can believe it, fire and ice, one tour apiece. Got wounded both places."

"Damn. I'm sorry."

"Part of the deal, old woman. I was supposed to get killed. You ever see those old movies about the Nazis, where they used to scare soldiers by threatening to send them to the Russian Front? That was me by the end; I was on all their undesirable lists, so they kept sending me places where they sent anybody expendable. Surprised them by not obliging, so they brought me home and put me on some of the more drop-dead evil crowd control, when things got bad around the capitol. I guess you can even call me a war criminal, really. Not proud of any of that, but hey, you get used to going where they say. It can take a while to start drawing any moral lines." Mo took another drag, coughed it out. "I guess they did me a favor by kicking out the queers. Kept me from wearing the uniform when they stopped pretending they believed in any rules at all. Kept me from the shame of looking back on the kind of things I might've up and cooperated with."

"We've talked about this before," Lise told her. "You would've drawn the line."

Affection flashed in Mo's smile, but it was the affection a mother has for a child who has said something impossibly naïve. "I love you for saying so, but I occupy this skin and I'm seriously not anywhere near that confident about my nobility."

"I know you. There are places you won't go."

"I know *me*, babe, and there are places I *went,* when I was one of them, that argue otherwise. Even places I *went* when it finally came down to fighting for our side that argue against any portrait of me as anything but a murderous shit."

She was distant, for a while, staring at her own reflection in the dark TV screen, focusing on that image of herself as if she expected it to stand up and start acting out its own drama, independent of the woman it pretended to be.

"It's like Miss Daisy, here, was saying about her boy, whatsisname. I promise you, he'd act the same way he did before if the political winds ever switched back. People learn nothing, for the most part. Any time it looks like they're getting better, either as individuals or a group, it's just a hiccup."

"You're more than a hiccup," Lise said.

Mo only shrugged. "A belch, maybe. You make me want to be a better person, so there's that, at least." She offered what was left of the joint to Lise, who shook her head. Taking it back, she stuck it back between her lips, and left it there without inhaling, the smoke drifting past her eyes as she stared at the blackened screen. After a few seconds, she said, "That what you wanted to know, old woman?"

"Not all," Greta said. "Who did you lose?"

"I was in uniform. Lost a shit-ton of people."

"That's not what I meant, and you know it. You're going to the Dedication. Who exactly did you lose at home?"

Mo turned toward her. Lise saw only the back of her head, but knew the face well enough to know exactly what resentment was flaring in those dark brown eyes, what message of *Mind your own business, I'm not here to entertain you,* was being flung Greta's way. But she also perceived what anybody who didn't know Mo might have failed to, the subtle slump in her rock-hard shoulders.

"Shit-ton of people there too," Mo said. "My father. My sister Kylie. My brother Andy. About a dozen others I could put a name to, along with about a dozen more who were new to me, some of them kids. The racist little shit came into their Baptist church first thing on a Sunday morning, and sprayed the pews until two ladies from the choir tackled him. It was just about my whole goddamned life, the best part of it, gone in two minutes without warning, because he happened to have a bug up his scrawny little ass, and of course, the bodies weren't even cold before those True fucks got on the air and started saying, fucking hoax, it never happened, there never were people by any of those goddamned names, just crisis actors saying there were. That happened a year after I got drummed out, after my service record was wiped, after they said it was illegal for me to even say I ever wore the uniform, and so I had nothing left at all, not being a kid and not being an adult. It was like I'd just beamed down without ever taking a breath on this planet before. I'm going to the Dedication because that's a lie. Because they existed, and I existed, and I won't let anybody say otherwise. Is *that* enough?"

What impressed Lise most about Greta right then was her refusal to either look away, or do what other well-meaning people often have, make the moment about her own bottomless compassion. She just held Mo's look, and held her hands palms up, in what amounted to a shrug.

"My husband Dan," she said. "My son Freddie."

"My daughter," Lise said.

"Everybody who didn't make it," Greta said.

Then she got up and headed for the connecting door.

Lise almost told her she didn't have to go, but the tension she saw corded in Mo's back stopped her. Maybe, she thought, it was really better to end the night here, before more things got said that likely should not be said. And so it fell to her to be silent while Mo surprised her by speaking the words that were more likely to have come from herself, in her traditional role as peacemaker.

"Hey, Miss Daisy. I didn't say you had to go."

Greta's smile was soft and sad. "I didn't say you did, cuddlebug. But I'm going to have to at least try to get some sleep, and these days it always takes me some time to shut the thinking down. Good night."

"Good night."

The door clicked shut behind her.

Lise regarded the door for a bit, imagining the routine of the old lady on the other side, and feeling a little let down now that she was gone. When she turned back she found Mo's eyes, calm and measuring.

"That," Mo said, "is one balanced soul."

It wasn't the kind of phrase Mo used often. "You think so?"

"I ain't saying it's balanced in a happy place. She's like one of those rock formations you find in New Mexico, Arizona, places like that; big flat boulder teetering on top of a pointed one, looking like it wouldn't take more than a strong wind to knock both down. But it's balanced. I don't know what she had to go through to get herself there, but it is."

Lise felt a surge of warmth. "I always felt that way about you, Mo."

"Naaah, babe. I'm as unbalanced as a dog on its hind legs. It's amazing enough I can just hold that position, but every minute I keep it up is a fresh accomplishment."

• • • •

The weather took a turn for the worse. The weather reports said it would continue to, all day, and they didn't want to be delayed any more than they'd already been; so rather than stop for breakfast they contented themselves with the free donuts and coffee in the lobby, and hit the road at speed. The sky got uglier and uglier the more time they'd spent on the road. By noon the skies just opened up and they'd drove through rainstorms so severe that for a while it was impossible to see as far as the end of the car's hood.

At one point, a marveling Greta said, "The world's ending."

It was pretty much the only thing she said all day, that was not the delivery of necessary information.

"That's a pretty intense hyperbole, Miss Daisy."

And that was pretty much the first full sentence from Mo.

By one o'clock it became clear that to stay on the road much longer was to risk getting killed before they made any further appreciable progress toward their destination, and that as motivated as they were to get to the event on time, it really did make sense to find somewhere to wait out the worst.

It was not until 1:30 that they followed the signs off an exit to a family-style restaurant. Parking as close as they could to the front entrance, they still got drenched on the way in and shivered under the air conditioning as the waitress, a woman Greta's age with hair of an orange tint that did not exist in nature, brought them their laminated menus.

Lise took one look at the prices and made a snap decision. "Order what you want. This one's on us."

"You're just giving me a ride, dear. I didn't exactly require you to adopt me."

"Tough shit," said Mo. "We have, at least for the duration of this trip, and you damn well better get used to it."

Greta blinked. "I...okay. Thank you."

"You're welcome, and what was that stuff you said about the weather, anyway?"

It took Greta a second to figure out what was being referenced. "That the world's ending?"

"Yeah, that."

"It must have been a local thing. When I was growing up, my aunt used to say it all the time, any time it started raining hard at all. It was Armageddon every day the clouds burst. It became part of my personal vocabulary. Dan used to tease me for it. 'The world's ending again?' he'd say. '*Fourth time this week!*' Up until the day I guess you could say it did."

"Does for everyone," Mo said. "Some faster than others."

They ordered. A chicken salad sandwich for Lise, a big sloppy bacon cheeseburger for Mo, melon for Greta. They dried, and as they dried they lightened up. Mo told her favorite clean joke, in Lise's extensive experience her only clean joke, the one about two drunks and the tall Chicago building with strange aerodynamic qualities. Lise told a joke which, as per her regular habit, she blew completely, occasioning a lecture by Mo on the proper way to set up and deliver a punchline. Greta told affectionate stories of her sons, both her sons, doing cute things before reality intruded.

Throughout, Lise grew aware of a jowly man in his fifties, sitting sideways on his stool and paying more attention to the three of them than the conversation warranted. She did not know whether he was bored or what, but she took note of his interest in the way hard experience had taught her she would sometimes have to, in a world where any asshole at all could take offense at her being a woman or being queer or being with Mo; for just being, really. But then he looked away, at the wall-mounted TV set to a news channel, and she managed to tell herself that she was probably wrong about him; that he wasn't necessarily a Truer; that he was nothing like the one who had taken so much from her, not like him.

Then he erupted with words meant to carry. "Oh, Jesus. *This* snowflake bullshit."

The half-dozen conversations around the restaurant all cut off at once, as patrons craned to see what he was talking about.

The screen displayed an aerial shot of a great green field surrounded by trees, with the gray sliver that represented the edge of a parking lot just barely entering the frame at the lower left. From the air the structure at the center looked like any other irregular black shape, except that there was also a stage with red and blue bunting erected before it. The scattering of early arrivals manifested as tiny dots, here and there across the grass, a few of them so determined to keep their spots that they'd erected tents. The Chyron read, TWO MILLION EXPECTED AT DEDICATION.

"I mean, enough already," the guy complained, addressing the whole room as if certain it contained nothing but allies. "Get over it."

And as if through a filter of blood Lise saw herself standing, stepping away from the booth, and approaching the man, whose gaze was so firmly fixed on the screen that he did not see her coming until she was close enough to register in his peripheral vision. At which point his head swiveled on his neckless shoulders, and the two slitted eyes that had been regarding Lise and her friends with what she could now identify for certain as contempt, now found themselves obliged to register her as an immediate problem.

"Oh," he said. "I *thought* you looked like one of those."

Lise wanted to grab the fork now resting on his plate next to a half-eaten slice of pie, and drive the four tines into his carotid. Instead, she said, "Why is it bullshit?"

"I'm too smart to believe the fairy tales. None of it ever happened."

The communal gasp that followed did not rise from everywhere in the restaurant, but it came from enough of the diners that any impulse Lise might have had to back down or satisfy herself by merely cursing the man out, retired to where all unworthy impulses hide. "I had a daughter once. One of those fairy tales killed her. She says it's not bullshit." She jerked a thumb over her shoulder at the table she'd just left. "That old woman had a husband and a son. They say it's not bullshit. That bigger woman over there, she had a big family once. They say it's not bullshit. That's more than a dozen people whose ghosts are calling out *your* bullshit, just at the table behind me. Are you still willing to say it?"

"I can think what I want."

"Yes. You can. And what you want is to dance on the graves of people other people loved. So I want to know how you can sit there over a slice of pie and call our mourning bullshit. Explain it to me, mister. Show your work."

He rolled his eyes, because to him it was obvious that this was all still nonsense, self-evident to every other set of eyes that beheld it, and said, "Look, maybe it happened a few times, a crazy guy going berserk here and there. But not all those times people claim. That's just propaganda."

"Uh huh. And how many times are you willing to accept it happened? Five? Ten? Twenty? Just my daughter, my friend's son and husband, my other friend's family?"

"Jesus, lady. All I know is –"

Lise's heart was like a triphammer in her chest, the urge toward hysteria rising, but she could not tamp it back; the words can been summoned, and they demanded to be heard. "Exactly! *All you know is*! I'm so sick and tired of hearing people use that to hold on to whatever ignorant bullshit they believe! You start with your delusional nonsense and then more information comes in and you go straight to that battle-hymn of the sad and bigoted, *all you know is,* because it cuts off any new knowledge that might be in danger of disturbing your peace. Well, I say *all you know* is no excuse for being hateful, stupid and blind. We lost people! Why is that bullshit to you? I'm not leaving you alone until you tell me why, *exactly!*"

He leaped off the stool, and for a fraction of a second Lise was certain that he meant to strike her. She did not back off, in part because she didn't have time, and in part because she was angry enough to tear down the moon. But at the same instant he drew his fist back winding up for the blow that might have put her down, his eyes flickered upward, to a fresh presence just over her right shoulder. It unmanned him. He visibly faltered and returned to his seat, eyes down. "Bitches."

"Now," Mo said, "that's the first even halfway intelligent thing to come out of your mouth."

"I'm betting ever," Greta said, and this was enough of a surprise to Lise that she had to glance back over her shoulder to confirm it. The little woman had risen too, and though it remained likely, in Lise's estimation, that she'd have trouble breaking a twig, it no longer seemed like a proposition the average loudmouth would be willing to test.

Sometime during the past minute or so another man, thick-faced and jowly and wearing a short-sleeved blue shirt and a tie not nearly long enough for his height, had emerged from a back room to regard the tableau with a blank mask that did not seem to be taking any sides. The blowhard at the counter, casting about for allies, recognized him as his most likely rescuer and cried, "Yo! Mel! You gonna let these crazy women get away with harassing your customers?"

Mel did not leap into action. Instead he performed a slow blink similar to the one common among pet cats assuring their human caretakers of their capacity for boundless adoration, and said, "I'm thinking...yes."

A couple customers actually clapped at that.

The man at the counter could not believe his ears. "They started it!"

"And finished it, too, looks like. I approve." Mel's bland features twitched, then flickered away from the man. "Ladies. I'll be around with your check in a minute or so."

It was a clear cue to de-escalate, but Lise didn't head back to the booth until Greta tugged on her wrist, murmuring that this had gone far enough. She permitted herself to be dragged back, but even once seated she kept her eyes fixed on the man at the counter, who had managed to recollect some of his prior arrogance and was spending it on a smirk and a long, sad, knowing roll of his eyes.

Not one word of hers, or of Mel's, had penetrated his shield of rock-hard certainty. *All he knew, was.* All he thought he knew, at this one moment, would always be the absolute sum total of his philosophy, forever untouched by any experience or data or input from others; any rage he ever encountered anywhere would be just another reason to believe he was right. The opposition would forever be proof of it, and he would go to his grave unchanged, no matter what passed between now and then.

Mo told Greta, "If it ever occurs to you to wonder how someone like me wound up with someone like Lise, it's because she can do that. She's a stealth badass."

Greta said, "You should probably be more careful about letting her read in peace."

"Probably," Mo replied. "But what's the fun of that?"

The man at the counter muttered, "See if I eat here again," tossed a bill down, and departed.

Greta watched him go, into an afternoon that had returned to bright sunlight, and said, "We should wrap up. A guy like that might come back with friends."

"Old woman," Mo said, "I am in the mood to most sincerely hope so."

That was when Mel returned, alongside the orange-haired waitress who had served them, and said, "Ladies. I may not look like much, but I actually agree with that."

"Okay," said Mo, in the wary tones of someone still waiting to see where he was going with this.

"I take it you're going to the Dedication?"

Lise said, "You take that right."

"I guess there's going to be a memorial wall or something? Something people will use to put up pictures of the people they lost?"

"I guess so. Why?"

He took out his wallet and removed a dog-eared, much-handled school photo of a smiling little boy, about ten years old. This he handed to Lise, who saw at once that the boy had not been exceptionally cute, had not even photographed all that well; in the image recorded here, he looked sleepy and heavy-lidded, and his smile looked forced, in the familiar manner of anyone whose better qualities remained stubbornly invisible to any camera lens. He had been a kid who did not know how to pose, whose only tolerable photos would forever be candid ones.

But the resemblance to the man who'd just handed Lise the photo was undeniable.

"That's my boy Jerry," Mel said, with surprising shyness. "It wasn't his best picture, but it was his last one anyone ever took. I'm not up to the ceremony, myself, but you'll see to it that he gets where he needs to go."

Lise didn't hug the man, but her voice caught in her throat when she said, "Of course."

"Your meal's on the house. If you stick around long enough for us to pack something to go, so's the next one. I want you to get my boy there."

●　●　●　●

With supplies in hand, they made up the day's lost time by driving past dark, but by about eight they hit catastrophic delays. They became part of an endless constellation of red brake lights, crawling on grid-locked roads.

Mo turned on the radio to see if there'd been an accident or something, and found a report establishing that nothing waited up ahead but more stoppages. Several of the major highways that converged on their destination were already experiencing two to three times their usual daily traffic, and even the feeder roads were well on their way to becoming parking lots. Some were expected to close. So many people had gone early that the site would reach peak crowd capacity a full twenty-four hours ahead of the event. Pleas were being issued to people who were merely sympathizers to get off the road and give priority to the bereaved. It was a good idea, but, as the commentator said, even that measure would not come close to being enough. The crowd was already going to top a million, and the site wasn't meant to accommodate more than half that.

It was not going to get any better. Almost everybody knew people among the dead; almost everybody was in some way intimately involved.

By about 9 PM, they were mired in an endless line of cars extending as far as they could see, and the news came over the radio that the main highway to the site had just shut down, and that this was putting extra stress on the routes remaining. The chance of making it to the event was dwindling to zero.

Lise said, "I'm beginning to think we're not going to get Jerry there."

"Maybe not to the Dedication," Mo said. "We might have to wait that out. But we're not headed home until we see the monument. Maybe a day or so later."

"It'll be a shame not to be there. To make ourselves heard."

"On the day, yeah. I'm a little broken-hearted too, babe. But it's not like whatever gets said tomorrow won't ever need anyone saying it again."

Lise said, "I don't want to fail my daughter again."

"Don't start that shit," Mo warned. "You didn't fail her the first time."

"It feels that way."

"Of course it does. You're her mother. It's the way you have to feel."

There was silence for a bit, in a cosmos populated by brake lights.

Then Greta said, "I'm thinking of any emergency vehicles that might have to get through, if anything happens. Our stubbornness could very easily have a body count."

And that decided it, though it was a while before they were able to pull off their surrender.

Hours of torturous start-and-stop crawling later, they achieved an exit and got the hell off the highway, following their GPS program another thirty miles through local roads to the first lodging, a courtyard chain, that had any remaining vacancies. The lobby was full of similar refugees from the road: some of whom hadn't sprung for a room but had settled on couches, or in the bar, where their conversations were so similar to one another that, passing among them, Lise got the impression she was listening to one group mind speaking in a hundred voices. Some of the pilgrims wept, some talked about making another try in a few hours, some said they would arrive in spirit. Some castigated themselves for starting too late, and there was the sense that they believed they'd betrayed whoever they were going for, whatever tragedy needed commemoration at the event.

They could not get two rooms this time. They got one with a single queen-sized bed, and as they filed into the room, Greta hung back, regarding it with open discomfort.

"I can take the recliner," she offered.

"No, you can't," Lise said. "We'll share the bed."

"Come on, that's really too much."

Mo said, "You're gonna have to stop saying things like that, Miss Daisy. We told you already, you've been adopted. And not just for this trip, either. When this is done, we're not letting you back to living in some car."

"You're…"

"We talked about it, last rest stop. Whoever we are now, whoever you were before the shit touched you, we're relations now. People like us got *made* family, in blood and fire. There'll be room for you, in our home and in our life, if you want it, however long you want it."

"We elected you house Mom," Lise said. "We don't let the house Mom sleep in her car."

Things got weepy for a while after that. They hadn't gotten weepy when Greta talked of her kids or when Mo talked of her murdered family. They got weepy now, not to the point of wailing hysterics, but certainly to the point of shiny eyes and broken thanks, and it wasn't long after that the three of them were sharing the bed, watching the live coverage of the highways.

The congestion might not have been so bad had the Dedication taken place when people were merely sick of losing their sons and daughters and mothers and fathers and husbands and wives to acts of madness in public spaces; there had been rallies a-plenty back then, and some of those had drawn hundreds of thousands.

But back then nobody had lived in a world where even talking about it was a crime. People had been told again and again that it was somehow not yet time to talk about it, that it was "too soon." People had been told that they were crisis actors and their own lost sons and daughters the fabulations of the propagandists, but they had not been arrested for saying the names of their children or for eulogizing them in sentences that also included the words "shot," or "gun." True America had done everything it could to bury that heartbreak beneath its laws and the resentment had grown and grown until there was nothing left for it to do what all substances under pressure do, which is erupt; and now the roads were lined with people who had been shut up, sidelined, mocked for their tears, and refused the right to speak. In all those tens of thousands of brake lights there were those who had been rendered mourners by random maniacs, and those who had been granted that status by state-sponsored purges, and those who had earned their own place in the parade by losing still more during the inevitable fight to put True America down.

Mo muted the picture and said, "We should have started earlier."

Lise said, "Yeah, maybe we should have," and she didn't only mean the drive.

The picture switched to an artist's rendering of the Monument to the Denied, an arrangement of black razored peaks stabbing upward at an improbably blue and cloudless sky. Little dots around the base, representing people, established the equally improbable scale of the thing, mindblowing really when one considered just how many of the offending weapons had needed to be melted down to contribute to it. But to look at it was to look at the sheer scale of the tragedy that had raged for so long; the one that the leaders of True America had said was anti-constitutional to even talk about. How could there have been so many? And how many were still in cupboards, in safes, in the secret possession of lonely figures who had nothing to live for but some spasm of public rage?

And on that line of scrolling text, at the bottom of the screen:

The University of Texas at Austin, 17 dead, 1966…Salem Oregon, 5 Dead, 1981…Jacksonville Florida, 6 dead, 1990…Killeen, Texas, 24 Dead, 1991…Long Island, New York, 6 Dead, 1993…Columbine, Colorado, 15 dead, 1999… Virginia Tech, 33 dead, 2007…

Lise felt her private grief, the part of it that belonged to her and no one else, swell to a terrible all-encompassing phenomenon. The scale of it, always understood intellectually, always a lump in her throat, was suddenly too much to process.

She scrambled off the bed and ran to the bathroom, where she tried to vomit but failed.

She didn't need the scrolling text. She could name the ones that inevitably followed herself.

Aurora, Colorado, 12 Dead, 2012…Newtown, Connecticut, 28 Dead, 2012…Orlando, Florida, 49 Dead, 2016…Las Vegas, Nevada, 58 Dead, 2017…Parkland, Florida, 17 Dead, 2018.

All those that had followed, the casualty counts of the worst rising into triple digits and--in a few cases involving organized groups—past one thousand.

Nowhere on that list, she knew, was the one that had started her on this journey. It didn't have a name, or even a body count. The one that hadn't been a *mass* shooting at all.

She waited for the false comfort of purging, until she knew that it was never happening, and after a bit rose and went to the sink, where she studied her own wan face in the mirror and decided that she was with company that would not care how she looked.

By the time she returned, both Mo and Greta were on their feet waiting for her.

Greta said, "Are you all right?"

Lise shook her head. "I may look okay, I may even act okay, but the answer to that is never, *ever* going to be *yes*. That's why you'll never hear Mo ask me that. She knows."

"Honey, I saw you take on that ignorant fool at lunch. You were not just okay, you were *magnificent*."

"And it was not me being *okay*," Lise told her. "I *wanted* to stab him in the neck with a fork. I don't think confronting him accomplished anything, and I didn't feel any better afterward. If you two weren't with me, when he made his move, I might have run out of there screaming."

"But we *were* there, cuddlebug. And you kept *us* from running out of there screaming. You spoke for Mo, and me, and even that man Mel. You were stronger than you think. For us, and for your daughter."

Behind her, Mo said, "Greta."

Lise had stiffened. It wasn't the first mention of her daughter since Greta joined them, but it was the first to arrive when she felt like she felt now, and it almost sent her to the ground wailing. But she'd done so much wailing in her life, and it would not do to wail more in the presence of these women who had known agony just as terrible but not quite the same as hers, nor to punish the sweet Greta for something she could not have known.

And so she put trembling hands on the base of her sweater and pulled it up just beneath her breasts. The scar left by that one round was a single ugly pucker with a sharp extending line that ran from one side of her belly to the other.

Greta's hand flew to her mouth.

Lise explained in a cold, steady voice. "All those people who got told their children never lived? For my beautiful baby girl, it was literally true. No such child was born. She never suckled milk. She never cried or laughed. I never got to hold her in my arms or even to know what she would have looked like, what kind of person she would have been. I never got to take a photo. She would have seen the light in no more than three weeks, and all I got to know of her was the way she shifted inside of me when I was flat on my back on the sidewalk and she was dying. The same shot that killed my daughter, fired by some random loser who hated women for saying no to him, also ripped out my womb and so that will always be the grand total of my lifetime experience as a mother. All I could ever do for her was go to this dedication, where everybody who gets there will be able to declare everybody they lost, where I could declare that *she* was real, too.

"So this is what you're getting into, Greta. You're welcome to live with us. But you need to know, I'm *not okay.*"

Greta was too thunderstruck to speak, but that's when Mo wrapped her arms around her, murmuring, "What makes you think anybody ever is, babe? Especially in this cruel world. Okay's never been more than a work in progress."

Lise laid her head against Mo's shoulder, and held on tight. This, she knew, would not make everything all right; it couldn't. The monument couldn't. Another voice added to a congregation of millions couldn't. But the remembrance was not insignificant. The remembrance *was*.

It was some time before she noticed that Greta was in the embrace, too.

CARDS ON THE TABLE

The two of them had been hanging out for three weeks. They didn't use the word "dating," because they weren't ninety for God's sake, but they did all the things that the process required, from eating dinner in quiet venues that encouraged soft and charming conversation, to putting aside hours that could be divorced from agenda and devoted to careful examination of whether they needed to have things to do, before they could be comfortable together.

There were also all the other expected things, from dancing at clubs too loud for conversation at less than shouted volume, extended and unplanned walks in places with grass and trees, shared encounters with delightful stray dogs, little acts of generosity and kindness and only fleeting moments of irritation.

This was it, they both thought. This would be the one.

He was some kind of writer and she was some kind of nutritionist, and the sex had arrived on schedule, not volcanic but certainly pleasant, its actual give and take rendered better by the considerable chemistry.

They got along.

They didn't speak the L-word and or the M-word, let alone that stiff C-word *commitment*, but all seemed in reach.

And then on schedule came the time for the talk.

They could have been at her condo, but today they were at his, a cozy but not cramped three-bedroom space that defined as rooms two spaces that should have been classified as closets. He had indeed used one of them for that very purpose, neatly stacked the arcana of his existence, mostly books. He had long since shown her mint copies of his four novels without doing anything as gauche as demand that she read them, but his many crates of contributor copies made her wonder about the special form of hell that awaited the prolific. Around them were various trophies in the shape of rocket ships and lucite blocks containing captive planets, testifying to his warm reception by his chosen field, and other objects that were not precisely art but were pleasant enough, even if her own tastes would have prevented their display in any room dedicated to the entertainment of respectable visitors. Still, she felt the fascination that went with knowing a person through the things.

Then he escorted her back to the living room couch, fixed her a drink designed to burn as it went down, and instead of curling up beside her sat in the director's chair opposite her, his brown eyes too earnest at a point in their relationship where neither the L-word nor M-word had yet been evoked. They all seemed to lurk in the near future, she thought; hell, she was beginning to hope. But there's a reason you cook chicken until all the pink is gone. Anything consumed too early in the cooking process can be toxic. As a nutritionist among other things, she knew this.

He said, "We need to talk."

Apprehensive, she said, "Do we?"

"I think so. Do you need a refresher on that drink?"

She didn't remember drinking it, but when she inspected she found that she had. "Yes."

He went. He came back. He watched as she took the required sip, and as she placed the glass on the required coaster.

She said, "Should I be worried?"

"I don't think so. We probably have a really good thing going."

"I'm not sure I like the sound of that 'probably.'"

"Neither do I. But I think it's time we let each other in on the things that need to be said now, before they have a chance to get awkward."

She said, "You're married. Or gay."

"I am neither."

"Then what do you mean by awkward?"

"We're having this conversation because I hope it won't be awkward. But you know how it is. The first few weeks you spend with another person are like a job interview. You behave extra well. You show your best side. You give them a chance to know the best version of yourself, before you mention anything that might risk a hard No if revealed too early.

She studied his face, which was wide-eyed and earnest, his emotions as open to her as a bloody gazebo in a park.

"You've been hiding something from me."

His head-shake could not have been less vehement. "I've been prioritizing. Giving you my best, before pulling out the…"

"…the not so good?"

"The part that would most benefit from being saved until later. I've never lied to you. I just didn't think it was time yet."

"You're a Republican."

He flashed a grin that lit up his face. "For that I would have waited another month."

She thought about it, considered making a big speech about honesty and openness and the impropriety involved in not going into this whole big routine until after they'd started sleeping together; and then she thought that for all she knew it might be a secret cross-dressing habit, or an allergy to peanuts. Neither one of them would have been a hard pass. And then she said, "All right. You go first. Get past that okay, and I might have one of my own."

He took a deep breath, and it was the kind of inhalation where you can see the oxygen make its way not just into the lungs but into the bloodstream, preparing the body for hard effort.

He said, "You know I'm a writer."

She said, "Yes."

"You know it's how I make my living. It hasn't made me a rich man. But my income from it is larger than you would guess, by a couple of zeros. And that's a good thing; I wouldn't be able to pay for this place from the occasional novella sale to ANALOG. I write the stuff because I love it. But I need to supplement my earnings from that with something else."

She threw out another guess. "You deal drugs."

He shook his head. "I write porn."

The eye contact was so pure, so much the look of a lost puppy in the early stages of learning that dropping a turd in the hallway carpeting was not a good idea, that she had to resist laughing out loud. "Is that all? My *little brother* writes porn."

"I know," he said, and this really was the first creepy element, because this happened to be a family secret that she had not yet gotten around to sharing. "But it's not normal porn. Not most of it. Let me get through this, okay?"

"Okay."

"I have an author account at all the usual online sellers. I upload a couple of e-books, all short-story length, every week. I've been doing it for a few years now. There are hundreds of them, already. They're steady sellers. The least popular sell as many copies as the average first-edition paperback. The most popular sell in six figures. There are readers who buy everything I write; some who support me under my pen name on GoFundMe and Patreon. It's a very good living. I'd love to make that kind of money with the fiction I write under my own name, the stuff I really care about, but it doesn't even come close. Pennies, by comparison."

And then he took another deep breath, looking for all the world like a man who expected her to fling her glass at his forehead.

She said, "This is adorable. I'm still waiting to be shocked."

"Well, you know how Stephen King keeps thinking of *interesting ways to kill people.*"

"I don't read Stephen King."

"Yes, but you aware that there is a man called Stephen King, and that he writes horror novels, right?"

"I just don't like him."

"Yes," he said patiently, "but you know he exists, right?"

"Well, yes."

"Okay. He doesn't actually kill people. He's a very nice family man whose biggest eccentricity is a past substance abuse problem. Mostly he's just like any other horror writer. He's very very talented at thinking about things that seem too terrible to think about. Okay? And it makes him big money. I happen to be very, very good at coming up with extreme fetish porn. I come up with the most repellent forms of sex imaginable, and I write about them as if they're super-hot, and none of it really reflects the kind of relationship, and I want to make sure that you know that I do this, before you find out by accident."

"How, exactly, would you expect me to find out by accident? I don't do random google-searches for scheisse-porn."

He was visibly impressed that she could summon the phrase, but he recovered and went on. "Look, if it was just stuff like pony-play, or incest, or mind control, or anything like that, I wouldn't have hesitated so much to tell you. I'm telling you that all that stuff is downright hackneyed. Look up any of those kinks and you'll find pages and pages devoted to it, some of it clearly written by virgins because much of it is physically impossible. I'm telling you I come up with stuff that even the most extreme forums consider disgusting, and the more disgusting it is, the better it sells, the more money I make Every time I write another it's with the secret hope that I've finally gone too far. But it never happens. I wrote one about a man and woman who got themselves dosed with a super powerful aphrodesiac and are sewn up inside a dead cow rotting in a field; I called it BURGER KINK. Twenty thousand downloads. Another about a brothel entirely staffed by coma patients. I called it PIMPING THE BRAIN DEAD. Only eight thousand for that one. Another where Thomas Jefferson and George Washington take turns servicing each other anally. I called that one FONDLING FATHERS. I did one about a veterinarian who never saw a newborn kitten that didn't make him hot. You can guess the title of that one. I –"

"I get the idea. Honestly."

"I'm telling you. It started as a way to earn extra money. I didn't expect it to become a second bloody career, towering over the one I really care about. But it has, and if there's one thing I want us to be clear about it's that –"

"Ricard."

"--none of it's anything I would ever actually do, not in a million –"

"*Ricard.*"

He froze, like a child caught with his hand in his mother's lingerie drawer.

She said, "I *get* it."

"I didn't want you to think of me as some kind of, of…"

"It's fantasy," she said. "People imagine all sorts of things they wouldn't actually do. If everyone who read bondage novels actually had a harem of captive women beaten into compliance it would be some kind of national disgrace. Even the people who try to live the lifestyle in real life are mostly just pretending. I find it hilarious, myself."

"You've…read…"

"I'm large, Ricard, I contain multitudes. This dread secret of yours doesn't bother me at all. You don't have to worry about me being so scandalized by it that I flee back home to mother. It doesn't matter to me. I know you're a good man. Are we done?"

He got misty. He got up and came around the coffee table and kissed her, not passionately but with deep and profound relief, the sense he'd been hoping for that he'd found the blessing of acceptance at last.

She kissed him back, once on the lips and once on his cheek and then quite a few times in a few more interesting places, and only then that she drew back, and said, "Of course, it does go both ways."

"What?"

"You're absolutely right. If this relationship is to go anywhere meaningful, it does require full disclosure. Please sit down. In that chair."

He studied her for a bit, then went back to the director's chair on the other side of the coffee table, a certain apprehensive cast to his eyes.

She said, "Replenish your drink."

He complied.

"Drink some."

He complied, a gulp bigger than any he necessarily had to, and thus delayed whatever she had to say by the duration of his coughing fit.

Then she said, "Are you ready?"

"For anything," he said, gamely denying the contradictory evidence of his gag reflex.

She took a deep breath, let it out, and then said,

"I eat human flesh."

Whatever he'd expected her to say, it was clearly not that. "Excuse me?"

"Long pig. The most dangerous game. Meat that could once communicate in words. I've eaten it, I like it, and I'm not going to give it up any time soon."

More blinks from the writer of extreme porn. "What?"

"Look. For a while there I majored in anthropology. I had a professor who had spent some time in the Amazon, among tribes who had never been contacted by anybody else. One was almost as hostile to outsiders as India's North Sentinelese, if you know who they are – killed anyone who ever encroached upon their territory, that sort of thing. Very dangerous people, but with a certain charm, if you got to know them. They weren't fanatics about it or anything. They didn't take captives frequently enough to subsist on the stuff. Mostly they ate what everybody else in their part of the world would find to eat. But they believed that human flesh had great power and they thought it was good for the soul to have some, maybe once or twice a year, if only to commemorate ceremonial occasions. That much, they could supply."

He said, "You're not kidding."

"My professor friend attended one or two of their feasts and joined them. I see it as probably thinking he had a choice between being at the table or being on it. He said that what they made was greasy, but good for the digestion. Later, he returned to America and found himself missing the stuff. So he found a dealer and started inviting the students who he thought he could really trust."

His mouth opened, then closed. "D-did you know before you… you…?"

"Please. There's an unwritten rule. You don't trick people into putting anything into their bodies that they wouldn't ingest willingly. My professor screened his dinner guests very carefully. He told them what he proposed to serve, and he explained where he had gotten it. He made sure that everybody knew that no one had been killed for the purpose of supplying his pot; they were all people who had been expected to die already and were willing to take a generous payment in exchange for donating their bodies to science. He always took the prime cuts and gave the anatomy lab what was left. Very above-board. Nobody got hurt. The students he invited, the ones who said yes, all agreed that it was quite good. A couple said that it was the kind of thing you eat only once, just to cross it off the list; a couple said that they might indulge in invited again, but that it was not something they would ever shop for themselves; a couple, like me, absolutely adored the flavor and decided to make it one of their staples. I have it about once or twice a month, now."

"You're a cannibal."

"Not exclusively," she said. "I don't have the resources to do any more than that. It's expensive stuff, and you don't want to keep dealing with suppliers who might be stocking their shelves any which way. I can tell you stories. There's a whole illicit market in teen runaways. They're very tender. Like milk-fed veal, I guess. My professor got a couple of his dinners from suppliers like that, which is one reason I changed my major and stopped talking to him. I'm not evil and I'm not crazy. No, what I get is from hospitals. Fresh autopsies, mostly. Kidneys and livers, mostly. A little bit gets taken off the top when the pathologist does his thing. Or amputated limbs from car accidents and the like. Nobody cares about what happens to their leg when they're done using it. Why let a perfectly good leg go to waste when it can be put on the grill?"

"Please," he said, the tip of his tongue protruding from between his white teeth.

"Come on," she said. "It's like I tell you: it may be technically against the law, but it's not taking advantage of anybody. There's no operation to breed people for the purpose. There's no ranch where the souls who end up on our mill around naked, being herded in and out of corrals and waiting to get branded on the buttock. There's no ramp to an industrial slaughterhouse where they get beaned on the skull with a sledgehammer. I can't say that there's never been such a thing, but it's not the kind of place where any of my contacts get supplied. It's just what I say: the scraps that were going to get thrown out anyway. Which is safer anyway, since what I eat is certified chemotherapy-free, tested for mercury and heavy-metal buildup, and totally organic. And if it comes down to that, it is just meat, a kind of meat that people have been eating for as long as there have been people on this planet. When expertly prepared, it's downright exquisite. I enjoy it. Is that so wrong?"

He had become very, very quiet and very, very green.

"Say something," she commanded.

He required three attempts to speak. "You've made dinner for me. More than once."

"Oh, Ricard. Please. We have to trust each other. I have the same rules my old Professor had. I won't ever try to trick you. I won't include you in any of those meals unless you express an interest. It's just like you said...we have to know each other."

"I...was at your place, last weekend. You were out doing errands. You weren't going to be back for a while. I had to make myself some lunch. I found a can among the soups. It had a label, but no words on it. Just a baby's face. No way of telling what it was. I put it back on the shelf and ate something else. W-was it..."

She repeated his words. "You put it back on the shelf?"

"I thought it was concentrated milk or something."

"But you put it back on the shelf."

"Yes. I had Campbell's Chicken Noodle. Was that can really a b-b..."

"No harm done," she said. "When we move in together, I'll show you which cans to avoid."

He had fallen to regarding his shoes.

She got up and came around the table and placed her soft hands on his shoulders, before leaning over and kissing him twice, once on the top of his head, and once on his cheek. "It's okay," she murmured. "I know it's a little hard to take in. But you were right. This life we're headed for, if you still want it, it can only be hurt by secrets. It's good to share things and get them out in the open, so we can concentrate on what's important. Like loving each other. Like all the great times we're going to have."

He said nothing.

She said, "I just said I loved you. Do you love me?"

It took him a few seconds to answer. "Yes. Yes, I do."

"You don't want to call the whole thing off?"

"No," he said, with shaky wonder. "No. I don't. I just..."

"You just have some adjustments to make."

"Yes."

Her kiss reflected a deep and ravenous ferocity. "Understood. Finish your drink."

He did just that. Emptied the glass in less time than it would have taken to say it, this time without a coughing fit. He thought things about couples he had known, where the guy lived for Tarantino movies and the girl would put nothing on the screen, ever, but *Love, Actually*. Where the girl loved to ski and the guy had an intolerance for a cold that led to long cocooned afternoons, watching the streets turn white and imbibing mug after mug of hot chocolate. Where one of the two would adore a band capable of making the other projectile hurl. None of these differences needed to be irreconcilable. Against them all, one always had to consider the smile that lit up your day, the morning breath that was terrible but that you didn't really mind, the rhythm of a soft heartbeat, transmitted through bare skin. *Life*, he thought, at first a little desperately, and then with still-shaky but nevertheless renewing conviction. *It was never going to be an exact fit.*

He more-or-less believed it by later that evening, at around the time they finished making love.

It was perfect. It was if anything better, now that they'd both unburdened themselves. It was, god help him, if anything delicious. A moment that could lead to a wonderful life.

The only bad moment was afterward, in the pitch-black darkness, when they were drifting off to sleep and she slid the negligible distance across the sheets to tuck her forehead into the space at the base of his neck.

"You know," she whispered, in a voice that reeked of invitation, "Fair is fair. I think it would be only reasonable for me to check out some of your hot porn."

He could tell, from the expectancy of her silence, that he was expected to reciprocate.

But instead, he pretended that he'd already tumbled into dreams.

THE END OF THE WORLD, MEASURED IN VALUES OF N

Listen.

The world ended thirty seconds ago.

You greet this whisper with incredulity. After all, here you are, living and breathing. The people around you are living and breathing. You might be drinking coffee in lying in bed trying to decide whether to get up. You are reminding yourself of all the little life tasks awaiting you, things that need to be taken care of in order for you to continue going about your day. Thoughts of the apocalypse are a thousand miles away. Lunacy, they seem.

Then the voice clarifies.

The precipitating event, the one that is going to end the world, took place thirty seconds ago. Somebody pushed the doomsday button. A comet struck the other side of the planet. The first zombies started rising from their graves. The common cold developed a spontaneous mutation that is airborne, 100% communicable, and 100% fatal. The sun just went nova. Alien intelligences turned their cold and pitiless eyes toward this little planet, intent on incinerating us with heat rays from their ambulatory death machines. A perfectly nice young married couple planning their first child just conceived the most ruthless genocidal madman in all human history. Somebody just got funding to create a black hole in the laboratory. Whatever it was, people, the event that we might have been able to prevent, had we only been given a tad more warning, has taken place within the last thirty seconds.

It's not just coming. It's here, and it's too late to ameliorate the consequences: The world has ended, and what remains, for however long it takes, is the packing away of the toys and the putting out of the lights.

That's the given. That is the news being delivered to every human being, by the same whisper, at this moment.

Assume that the voice speaks with authority, and that there is no room for doubt.

Now it tells you how much time we all have left, before the process already begun reaches its completion, and the last of us are gone.

Call this value N.

How does humanity react, for different values of N?

· · · ·

If N is two seconds,

there is time for everybody to unleash a single shouted exclamation. More people will say, "Jesus!" or "Oh, Shit!" or their local equivalent than at any other given moment in the history of the world. Some people will have time to utter their chosen phrase and will then immediately repent, thinking of things they should have said instead; and this thought will have just enough time to cross their minds before they say the equivalent of, "No, wait," or, "I mean . . ." But after that, the time will be up.

· · · ·

If N is sixty seconds,

what people do will depend entirely on whether they're alone. Some will embrace one another. Some will scream, some will pray. Some will turn to their loved ones and utter a few words of deep appreciation, or of apology. Some will turn to the people next to them and do the exact opposite, hurl the punch that was always, before this, held back for fear of consequences. There will be some murders, some suicides, a tribute in both cases to fast thinking. People on high balconies will indulge a lifetime dream of flight. Chaos, the kind of chaos that can happen when there's prior assurance that the bill will never come due, will have time to erupt; but it will only have time to start, not to go anywhere of genuine consequence.

Still, it's more time than you think. Try holding your breath.

• • • •

If N is one hour,
then all places of business will empty, as people hit the elevators and the staircases in a desperate hurry to get to their loved ones. The roads will clog with traffic jams as people who should have known better try to accomplish a commute that was forty-five minutes even on good days. More sensible people will grab their telephones, and though the grid will fail, many final words will be spoken, by those separated by distance; loving words and spiteful words, and there will be infinite passing of secrets by those who held them close to their breasts, waiting for the right moment to tell those important to them that Uncle Bob is their real father, that they are sleeping with Nazir, that they were the one who took Aunt Bella's tea set, that they are gay. There will be shooting sprees and there will be rapes, committed by those who have always feared prison but now say, why the hell not. There will be lots of perfectly acceptable last-minute sex, though some will start too late and not get to finish and others will start too early only to face a rumpled bed and the apocalypse as literal anticlimax. Some of that sex will be between minor acquaintances with no time to get to anyone they're actually involved with, who will seize those they've occasionally daydreamed about and say, "The faculty lounge! Now!" Many will spend the entire hour weeping; a few will spend it grinning at the panic taking place all around them and exult that the sins they've kept secret their whole lives will never bear consequences. In the first few minutes, several nations with nukes will say to hell with it and launch them, full commitment, because Chekhov's rifle must be fired, right now, if it is indeed true that the play's about to end. By the end of the hour, so many will have died that, depending on how the missiles fall, there might even be serious dispute over whether the absolute end had a greater body count than the end that came before it. That is, if there were anyone around to do the disputing.

• • • •

If N is one day,
many more people will commit crimes that require some planning and effort. Scores will be settled, not because it matters anymore, but because there is still minimal chance of being punished. It will a bad day, worldwide, to be a member of a targeted racial minority, or to be a woman; for that matter, to be a child. The nuclear exchanges will still happen, but they don't happen right away, not at the beginning of the day when the nations in question are keenly aware of how much time

they'll be cheating themselves of as well. Generally, it won't happen until the last hour.

Amidst the general savagery, though, you will be able to see other things. People who watch their calories binge. People who are on the wagon will fall off. People who have forgotten to smell the roses will try to make up for what they've lost.

Among all the feuds and vendettas erupting, there will also be any number of moments of personal grace. The son who hasn't visited his ailing mother for a while will ignore the excuse of the closed roads and spends the day making his way to her. The father who has estranged his daughter will do much the same, showing up at her front door even though he suspects that he will be rebuffed. People will play with their dogs. People will stay in bed to finish what they'll now know to be the very last books they will ever read. Neighborhoods will hold block parties that involve all the food and drink available because nothing has to be saved for later. There will be weeping but there will laughter. There will be a determined, defiant effort to it all, a quest to experience everything that can be enjoyed in one day, and among more people than you would guess this will not be an exercise in celebrating the worst, but in practicing the best.

The day will ring with intervals of human beauty.

And everywhere people will play the game of, "What if?" What if the warning had come earlier? What if they now had a week, instead of a day? How much more could they have done, with the time that was left?

● ● ● ●

If N is one week,

then in many places, civilization will fall faster and more catastrophically than could hardly be believed. It won't happen everywhere, but there are any number of tribes that will hold on to the offenses committed against them by other tribes, and with one full week to explore this history at length, will indulge grudges at length. The carnage will become organized, in many places Rwanda-style genocides that amount to a house-to-house purging.

You have heard the stories dating back to those times when the world was not ending and the perpetrators simply had no thought of justice ever catching up with them; now that the end is an absolute given, many places that stuttered to an uneasy peace, after past blood scourges, will work themselves up to replaying history in frighteningly short order.

Worldwide, anybody who's been suppressing criminality will indulge. People who can leave their cities will. They will head off for the mountains or erect tents in the woods or repair to the isolated little getaways they know about and hunker down, paranoid, intent on remaining alive until the very end. Others will stay in large centers of population, giving themselves over to service. Many are the civilians who will direct traffic, the belated Samaritans who will share what they have with others who don't have enough to make it to the end. When they hear of the terrible offenses being committed elsewhere, they will cluck in shame and ask the same question that people have always asked, but that will seem infinitely more pressing now: *At long last, what's wrong with people?*

· · · ·

If N is one year,
then humanity will for a while be no more savage toward itself than it has always been. People who would have run out and killed that son of a bitch Omar right away, if they knew that no punishment awaited, will now picture justice of a sort catching up with them, and refrain. After all, nobody will want to spend the last year of the world rotting away in prison, if there even are prisons being run, in the months to come.

No, it will be simpler, and more freeing, for many, to just relinquish the things that don't matter. People will sleep more. They will go on longer walks. They may keep their jobs, at least for a while, but they will stop thinking about where they're going to be and devote more thought to where they are. The marriages that need to break up will. The ones that were teetering for stupid reasons will stay alive. It will all be very relaxed and civilized, for the first six months or so, at which point the effort people were putting into making sure everything continued to work will begin to falter, and the last six months will become at first like the Wild West and then like the Barbarian Olympics of *Mad Max*.

Honestly, you thought it was bad when people only had one day to work this shit out. Give them six months to gradually relax into anarchy and the next six months, the next six months, will be an exercise in survival of the meanest. Some places will go like Jonestown and other places will go like Auschwitz. Other places, isolated places, will experience the discrete little apocalypse of the cocktail-swilling Australians of *On the Beach*. But generally? A year is precisely the wrong period of time. The end of everything will be imminent, but with time to think about it. And this is not a grand recipe for peace, given human nature.

· · · ·

If N is twenty years,
but you already know the answer to this one, don't you?

IN THE TEMPLE OF CELESTIAL PLEASURES

Jin left the last of his life's concubines sobbing in shallow water.

It was sad. He had loved the sweet girl as much as he was capable of loving any woman, which is to say that he had sometimes found himself giving thought to her wishes in the occasional circumstances where that did not conflict with his own.

Over the months since acquiring this last of his life's many distractions at the flesh markets of Tsau, he had kindly allowed her the useful fiction that she was a person and not an object, and had in that way encouraged her to see pleasuring him as not her duty but rather her most fervent expression of love. This was a helpful manipulation, in that it encouraged her to heights of enthusiasm that left the mere mechanics of her sexual training far behind. It was a little like praising a dog whose function was to serve as sentry and not as pet. The dog sincerely believes that it is being loved. The dog responds with loyalty and dedication to its purpose in life. Jin had whispered empty poetry in the girl's ear and accomplished the same result.

Her fate now that he was done with her was, of course, none of his concern, but he was not a wholly heartless man and so he regretted having to abandon her to a world where she would either starve to death before finding her way back to civilization or, once stumbling across one of the ramshackle little villages that dotted the edge of the frontier, likely fall under the power of some unwashed peasant not as benevolent as himself, and live the rest of her life being passed along between neighbors. As he packed up his camp, he even gave some thought to just doing the humane thing and cutting off her head, thus sparing her such uncertainty.

This took place at a hot spring by the base of the mountains known as the Dragon Teeth, six days past the trek across the valley of salt. He had taken her along to make that terrible part of the journey bearable, and—given the promise of this oasis on the other side—as something to amuse himself with for however long it took him to recover. It had been an arduous journey even for Jin, who had long ago exhausted all the diversions close to him and was well used to riding many leagues into uncivilized places, to find the pleasures that had not yet reached the Empire's capital cities; it had been an ordeal beyond belief for the girl, raised in isolation and fit only for service inside twilit, perfumed chambers. But she had provided acceptable companionship along the way, and rendered the days that followed a little bit of an idyll, and so to reward her he'd made love to her one final time in the waters of the hot spring. Buoyant, weightless in truth as well as status, clutching his flesh with the hunger of a starving woman faced with what would likely be her last meal, she had used every trick in the sensual repertoire that constituted her life's only education to render herself too precious a jewel to abandon.

Alas, she now bored him. So he granted her freedom in a whisper, and left her weeping as he strode naked from the pool and set about packing together his remaining provisions. He left her a serpentine dagger in case she elected to kill herself, and a tiny pyramid of gold coins and a sack of dried figs in case she wished to attempt the trek back to civilization. Then he filled his saddlebags with the remaining provisions he would need for his journey to the Temple of Celestial Pleasures.

It was only when he was fully armored and ready to leave the little oasis behind that he deigned to look at the nameless girl again, and found that she had not stirred from her place in the bubbling pool, but instead remained where he had left her, eyes averted in a manner that was no longer trained submissiveness but instead sullen insolence.

He said, "Come now. There is no point in sulking."

The etiquette of the serving caste demanded that she bow and make the sign requesting permission to speak.

Instead, she said, "I do not sulk, my Lord. I simply see."

"What do you see?"

"I see the true reason you will always seek a passion greater than any human arms can provide you, and I know exactly why it will someday destroy you."

"Oh?" He raised a skeptical eyebrow. "Why?"

"You are broken, my Lord. You are empty, and incapable of feeling for anything, even yourself."

He barked a laugh. "You are not the first slave I have freed. Always you reveal the hatred you have harbored for those you once pretended to adore."

"It is not hatred, my Lord. My love for you is real. It is only my understanding that speaks. I know that if you were not broken in the way I describe, you would have seen past the differences between us and been warmed by the fire I feel for you. I, by contrast, can love, and I shall not rest until I feel that exquisite warmth for someone who deserves my devotion more than you ever could."

Words like these were not unknown to him. So he allowed a smile to pass his lips. "Perhaps I shall fail in my search. Perhaps you shall succeed in yours. Perhaps we shall meet again in the land where all beings go, and at that time share how our respective quests went."

She covered her delicate breasts with her hands, an expression of modesty that she had never before shown in his presence. "I hope not, my Lord. You have left me no choice other than wishing to never see you again, not even in the land of the dead."

These were words that once would have obliged him to carry out her summary execution. But she was right; she was now free, and entitled to opinions. So he rode off toward the mountains . . . but not before he retrieved the food had been about to leave for her, leaving only the dagger behind. Truth, he felt, comes with a price.

* * * *

Jin saw many wonders on his journey into the Dragon's Teeth: strange animal shapes that lurked behind rocks and dissolved into shadows as he drew closer; chasms that swallowed light and seemed to have stars beneath them; one place where raging water rushed up a sheer cliff wall to form an upside-down pool of churning storm clouds. On two occasions he was attacked by mountain tribes who might have presented a danger were they not starved wretches. Both times, they rushed him to take what he had, but what followed was not so much a melee as a massacre. Jin felt no sense of accomplishment at being the last to stand amidst the corpses.

For two days an illness wracked him and he was forced to halt his journey while he huddled in a cave, burning with fever. For those long hours he lost leave of his senses, forgetting where he was and how he had come to this place, instead playing host to his life's parade of lovers, either seduced with charm from those of his class or purchased in the marketplaces welcome only to those fortunate enough to have inherited a fortune as expansive as his own. The men, the women, the eunuchs; the children stolen from foreign lands; the curiosities disfigured for his amusement; the innovative creation of one merchant in Pau, who obtained his human wares in infancy, trained them all their lives in absolute darkness, and then released them into light only on the day they met their future masters, before blinding them with fire so they would have only that one sight to contemplate, forever. He remembered bribing a magistrate so that condemned prisoners could be forced to service him until he slit their throats at the moment of his greatest pleasure. He relived a lifetime of joys unspeakable and pleasures beyond imagination; objects designed to be inserted in the willing and others that the unwilling would writhe in agony trying to expel; the use of ointments that cooled or heated or released hallucinogenic vapors when the skin was heated by passion.

He recalled his honored mother protesting that all this dallying with slaves was all well and good, but that it was time he produced an heir and took his position managing the family fortune. He remembered himself tricking her into signing away her own freedom so he could experience the sin of incest. He saw her cursing his birth as he shipped her off to the provinces with instructions that she was to be set to labor in the fields.

He remembered meeting fellow adventurers of the flesh who taught him about the Temple of Celestial Pleasures and advised him that it was a place he should seek out only after he had exhausted all other forms of ecstasy beneath the dome of Heaven.

Always, in his delirium, the people he'd used and known crumbled into dust once he was done. Always he was left unsatisfied. Always he was left chasing the great pleasures of a world that, for all his willingness to try anything once, continued to prove itself too finite for one as high-born as himself.

Blackness gathered around him. Death seemed to clutch him in its skeletal hand. But then he woke covered with a crust of his own vomit, his head aching but clear. He felt only need. And so he rode on.

* * * *

He found the Temple occupying a narrow cleft in the mountains that showed the only green he had seen in many days. It was a sprawling palace with walls of gold that confronted the sunrise and returned it to the sky. Cascades of crystalline water flowed from the minarets at each corner, feeding shallow pools that surrounded the edifice on all sides, providing Heaven with a perfect reflection of itself. There was no possibility of taking his horse all the way to the front gate; the beast trembled in fear and would not approach any closer. So he slit its throat and made the final approach on foot, striding on the bejeweled path that was the only route between the placid reflecting pools.

The gate was an obscene bas-relief in which hundreds of miniature human forms coupled in combinations of two or three, or four, no two positions alike, all possible sexual combinations represented. It was the most intricate work of art Jin had ever seen with his own eyes, and it moved him not at all. Only when he pulled the braided silver cord beside that gate did he experience something that astonished him, for the gate did not lift or lower or swing open like a door or slide into some recess in the wall. It simply gave the impression of receding, in some direction that defied all the dimensions Jin knew.

Beyond stood a small army of men and women of exceptional beauty. There were representatives of all the races he knew, and some he didn't, reflecting every possible human tint from cream to ebony, every possible body type from squat to giant. Some were unmarked and others were covered with ink or brands. All were naked. All were flawless. All regarded him with frank sexual contemplation.

The only being wearing clothes seemed neither woman nor man, neither young nor old, neither of Jin's nationality nor any other. Slight in a manner that would have seemed alarmingly emaciated for anybody else, strangely devoid of pores, the hairless creature in an ankle-length white gown strode toward him and regarded him with eyes that possessed neither whites nor irises, but were instead orbs of glowing silver. "You are Jin," s/he said, in a voice that seemed to emanate someplace other than his/her lips. "I am Rhaij."

He found he wanted this creature, alien as s/he appeared, more than he had ever desired any lover in his life. "Yes."

"This," s/he said, "is the Temple of Celestial Pleasures."

His throat went dry, as he realized that for once in his life he did not know what he was privileged to do next.

"Are these," he waved his hands at the gathered specimens of physical perfection, "my choices?"

The inhabitants of the Temple tittered among themselves, as if he had just uttered something adorable enough to have come from an infant.

The skin over Rhaij's right eye wrinkled in what might have raised an eyebrow, had there been any hair there to form one. "You have made a common mistake, traveler. This holy place is not what many pilgrims imagine, a more exotic form of brothel with a greater selection of pretty whores to choose from. To be sure, it sometimes serves that purpose when such commerce facilitates the training of those you see before you. They are all still struggling to achieve the same state of total jaded surfeit that has rendered all terrestrial forms of sexual ecstasy so dry and empty for you."

Jin felt a desperate need to re-establish some command over the situation. "How do you know what I have experienced?"

"Perusing your memories is the simplest of all our capabilities. It's an invasive process, one you no doubt experienced as burning delirium, but it was necessary to determine your intentions before we decided whether to permit your entry, or turn you back. This is how we know that the mere sexual services of all those who inhabit these walls, splendid as they might be for most, would avail a man of your life's experience little but a moment's distraction; nothing worth every crime you have ever committed, every league you have traveled, every sacrifice you have ever made in the coin of either soul or flesh. It would be pathetic, like offering a scrap of bread to one who has known feasts."

"I was told you offered a pleasure greater than any under Heaven."

"We do, Jin. It is just not any form of sex you imagine. It is the consummation that all of these acolytes hope to achieve, once they have exhausted their capacity to achieve satisfaction with mere terrestrial pleasures. For those who have tried everything else, experienced everything else, and found the pleasures of Man wanting, what awaits is greater than anything known by any being who crawled or walked beneath this blue sky. We charge one price: everything you have. These terms are non-negotiable, and only full acceptance of them will admit you any further into the Temple."

"I brought enough with me to ransom kingdoms. If that is not enough, I can sign a promissory—"

Again, the acolytes tittered.

"This is another common error," Rhaij said. "Have you not seen our golden walls, the jewels set in every paving-stone? We have other sources for such baubles. We have no interest in the riches of your civilization, which are as far as we're concerned an irrelevant burden to which you are free to return, once we have provided what you came here to find. No; we seek to charge you nothing you own, but everything you have. Will you pay that price?"

Fear stilled Jin's heart for all of a heartbeat. Perhaps he had not exhausted all the options available to him. Surely there had to be some courtesan, somewhere in the seven kingdoms, who possessed tricks he had not yet encountered. But just entertaining this thought meant imagining a long slow slog back to the fleshpots of the emerald coast, where he would find himself browsing the same assortment, facing the same dull-eyed eagerness in the eyes of servant girls and boys raised to no ambition greater than someday being used by a Lord like himself. It would mean experiencing the same disappointments, again and again, to the point of long nights spent contemplating the momentary flash of pain that would bring relief seconds after he slipped some dagger into his sated heart. The idea of commencing the search again was more, he found, than his jaded soul could bear. So he seized the moment, aware even as he did that it was a form of suicide.

"Yes," he said. "For a taste of pleasure greater than any I have ever known, I will give up everything I have."

Half an hour later, they castrated him.

* * * *

By then, they had made him drink a substance that conferred calm on both body and mind, and he watched most of what came next from the remove of a theatre patron watching the acrobats do tricks for his amusement. Two female acolytes with sleek black hair, twins he was told, fed him a potion that guaranteed arousal, used their painted lips to bring him to the very point of release, then withdrew and produced a bladed device of a sort that reminded him of the towering version used in his home city to behead murderers and thieves. This one did not stand tall and feared in a public square, being no longer than a man's forearm, but it operated according to the same general design. It was no more than a rectangular frame enclosing a spring-loaded steel blade designed to be pulled along a grooved track, and then locked into position until it could be released to leap back into its prior location with a force terrible enough to shred whatever lay in its path.

One twin pulled the blade all the way back, and inserted the pin that held it in place. The other lowered the now-empty frame over Jin's rigid member, enclosing his testicles as well, to ensure that they would also be included in the excision to follow. The first twin took care to make certain that the part of the frame enclosing the blade now lay flat against Jin's belly. The other released the blade.

The beautiful twins offered him reassuring smiles with cheeks now sporting wide constellations of scarlet freckles. But the potions Jin had been given did their job. For a time, he felt nothing.

The pain arrived when the potions wore off.

There were days of it, an eternity of rage and madness that consisted of him pulling at the chains that bound his wrists and ankles, while smiling acolytes of various sexes drifted in and out of his opulent cell to administer more potions, force-feed him his nourishment, and clean up his blood and waste. Several advised him in exotic accents how deeply they envied his imminent journey, even as they dabbed cream on the ragged wound between his legs, trimmed the bits that didn't heal properly, and massaged what was left into something that was less a ruin than a rippled, unoffending absence.

At the same time, other important pieces of himself were taken. All of these vanished during his periods of sleep, to the point where twilight became a time to rage against the sun he could see setting behind his room's tinted glass. But darkness always came, and the soft light cast by the room's array of scented candles was never enough to prevent sleep from once again claiming him. He woke one morning with all his fingers and both his thumbs gone, his hands reduced to shapeless paws that would never be able to grasp anything again. He woke another day to find that he had lost his nose, and a day after that to find that his lips had gone as well. The acolytes were generous when it came to providing him with mirrors, and thus did not hide from him the awareness that these additional disfigurements had given him the mien of a grinning skull, with a bony crater in the center of his face and a leering, moist rictus below. Against the shock of such thefts, he almost missed the day when they removed his nipples.

He feared that they would move on to other parts of him, but this was apparently what Rhaij had meant by "everything he had;" the surgeries ended after that, and the acolytes began to rouse him from bed for walks around the flowered grounds. They were kind and they were loving and when he despaired, which was often, they kissed his cheeks and advised him that he had paid all he needed to pay. Many were the paragons of beauty who rested their heads on his shoulder, and the sweet voices who assured him that all would be well, while their stunning eyes wept in sympathy with his tears. Most of the time he regarded what they told him as pretty lies. But as he healed, and grew stronger, and grew

used to being fed by companions who still possessed hands, he found he
had no choice but to hold on to the hope his caretakers had offered him.

Weeks passed in this terrible way, possibly months.

Then when they judged him strong enough they led him down a
tiled path into a part of the Temple grounds he had never visited before,
where the tree branches hung low with cherry blossoms, and the birds
were iridescent things with songs so close to words that his tortured ears
insisted on arranging them into poems. Rhaij stood at the center of a tile
mosaic, head tilted in concern as Jin's handlers led him to a bench and
bade him to sit there. The stone felt cool on his bare buttocks, mocking
all the rage that burned within him. Naked acolytes, male and female,
stood behind her in two rows, hands folded before them in a ludicrous
concession to modesty, their faces all beacons of unreserved love for Jin,
who had been kind enough to come here and share his journey with
them.

Rhaij stood beside a locked chest of some substance finer than iron
that captured the light of the sun and seemed to imprison some small
part of it on its surface before reflecting the rest back. "In here," s/he said,
"we store everything you have freely given."

He turned his head away.

Rhaij continued. "I wish you to know that this chest contains properties that prevent the passage of time, and therefore the decomposi-
tion of flesh. The parts taken from you still live. Our collected wisdom
includes delicate surgeries capable of restoring all of it to your body, with
full function. You would be able to walk away with full function, without
so much as a scar. But if you elect to proceed past this point, we will take
what you have given as tribute."

Jin's speech was a distorted thing, robbed by his disfigurements of
many of its consonants. "What . . . use can you possibly—"

"It is not a question of what use we could possibly have for them. It is
a question of what use you can possibly have for them. After all, the experience you seek will render all terrestrial delights moot. We have therefore
taken away most of the instruments you used to give and receive pleasure,
as you will never need them again. We would have taken your versatile
tongue as well, but at this point believe that the chances of it ever again
being used in a lover's manner again to be laughable and remote . . . and
we do prefer you to retain some vocal clarity, so we can converse with you
in comfort. But this will be your final chance to turn back. If you elect
to move on, then what sits in this chest will never be returned to you . . .
and if you beg for its return, then you will never know the nature of the

exquisite pleasure this Temple is dedicated to celebrating. It is now your choice. No other explanation shall be provided until after you have made your decision."

Jin burst into tears, because he feared moving forward more than he had ever feared anything else; because he suspected it would hurt; and because he also knew that either option was a fast road to misery; a decision on what condition he would be in as he endured the hopeless days between now and the end of his life. At long last he said, "Go ahead and take them away, damn you. I'll go on."

A plump beauty with hair like fire stepped up and took the chest by the handle, disappearing down the garden path with it even as Jin restrained himself from calling after her to stop. It was like losing what that box contained a second time, and this time he experienced the loss without potions or the shelter of sleep. As the path dipped, he saw her sink beneath the curve of the slope, until only the red curls of her head bobbed above that amputating line, a setting sun that in seconds disappeared from view as well.

After far too long, he became aware of Rhaij kneeling before him, resting those long delicate fingers on his bare knees.

He said, "That . . . was a lie, wasn't it? You didn't really have a way to put it all back. Nobody . . . could put it all back."

Rhaij's silver eyes shone with a light that could have been anything from empathy to deepest contempt. "Is that why you made the decision you did?"

Jin's answer came as a surprise to him. "No. I made the decision that offered me any hope."

"Then you should know. The founders of the Temple are not of your world. We possess arts unsuspected by even the most learned savants under this sky. We have machines smaller than the tiniest gnats, which can swarm into any wound and knit it in seconds. We have fires that can burn longer than any hearth in any city walked by the feet of man. We have chariots that can carry us to place so high above the clouds that the sky is black and breath itself an unobtainable treasure. We could feed all this world's hungry and we could render your earth molten at a moment's whim. There is no miracle devised by your poor imagination that we cannot demonstrate, right here, right now, without but the smallest part of the knowledge at our disposal. But what interests us, Jin, what really excites our enthusiasm and motivates everything we do, is pleasure . . . and I assure you, we can deliver what we say."

Doubt wracked him. "How? I've done everything."

"Have you never heard that the climax, just the climax, of the common barnyard swine lasts five times longer than the entire act does for you who consider yourself the master of creation? Have you never imagined the torrent of raging sensation that governs the mating of eagles? Would your mind not shatter if you possessed even the slightest clue to the blinding light that, at the moment so many beings crave, enraptures the largest creature who swims your seas? And that, Jin, is just under this sky. In our travels, we have filled what you would consider entire libraries with the taxonomy of creatures who live beneath under other suns, who know sensations that dwarf anything you or any human being has ever been equipped to feel. The very greatest of these is what all these young people around you have dedicated their lives to earning. And this is what we are prepared to provide you, now."

"But just once," he said.

"This is not out of cruelty. You must understand: the part of the human animal that can accommodate such sensations is as capable of being exhausted as soil can be leeched of the nutrients that permit life to grow. This is the main reason you can only achieve solitary pleasure a limited number of times, relying on the same mental images first used to achieve arousal. It is the reason certain narcotic substances entice their first-time users with unimaginable euphoria, but after only brief addiction, leave them chasing relief while returning no satisfaction at all. And it is the reason you, who have known more passion than the vast majority of men, came to this place no longer capable of appreciating anything this world had to offer you. Experience the delight we can share, and you will long to know it again, every day for the rest of your life."

He managed a weeping, "Will I be able to remember it?"

"Yes. But your capacity to ever feel it again will have been extinguished."

He lowered his head, blinked away a wave of burning fire, and pictured ten thousand faces, all now dead or lost to him; none of which he had ever truly known.

He asked himself: what fool first called life too short? Those who live it know that it is rather an interminable march away from that which once delighted us; and were it half the length, or even a third, the joys that make it worth living would still not be numerous enough to fill it. Were it tailored properly, we would all die as toddlers, still capable of being delighted by shafts of sunlight.

At long last he said, "I would give even more to have this. My limbs. My senses. Every remaining day of the rest of my existence. I do not wish to waste any more time with discussion. I am ready."

"Yes," Rhaij nodded. "I can see that you are."

*   *   *   *

They carried him to a shadowy underground chamber and set him on a carved stone slab, his arms and legs spread-eagled and held in place by chains. There they shaved his head and commenced the insertion of hundreds of golden filaments, finer by far than any silk, into his skull. This was, astonishingly to him after everything else he'd been through, painless, even if it was time-consuming. He had little to think about in the gloom, until an acolyte he had never seen before entered through the arched doorway and knelt beside him, without disturbing the others in their work.

She was almost unrecognizable to him without the kohl-rimmed eyes, and with her lush black hair shorn to half its previous length; but it was impossible not to recognize the serpent tattoos that curled around her soft shoulders, or the constellation of freckles that curled about her delicate right breast.

He said, "You."

His final concubine betrayed none of the anger she had expressed on their last conversation. "It is good to see you again, my Lord."

He could not help being aware of how monstrous he must now appear to her, and how distorted his speech must sound to her ears. "You said that you never wanted to see me again."

"After today," she said with absolute calm, "I will not."

"What are you doing here? Have you become one of their acolytes?"

"No, my Lord. I was offered that sublime honor, but once they told me what joining this order entailed, I declined. It is not for me, I'm afraid. I find that the empty pleasures of the flesh, for their own sake, do not draw me in the same way that they draw you. In my new life of freedom, I desire to find only love."

"Then—"

"They are kind, my Lord. On the day they walked through the days and nights of your life and saw how and where you had abandoned me, they came in their mercy to rescue me. They offered me the choice of admission to their temple, and new life as one of their acolytes, or free transportation back to the city of my choice, with a name and enough wealth to keep me in comfort for the rest of my life. I chose the latter.

They gave me the name but asked that I stay on as their honored guest, long enough to witness your transformation and offer you comfort in this, the day you await what you have always sought."

"And you have stayed . . . out of revenge?"

She lowered her unpainted lips and kissed the smooth nubs that had once been fingers. "I need no revenge, my lord. This is but the last gift I give to he who knew not that he once commanded my most sincere love."

Jin swallowed, and for the next few seconds struggled with a feeling that he had never known, at any point in his eventful life. It was a cold presence inside him, like a lump; and it weighed him down, like a heavy meal that he could neither digest nor pass. After a few seconds, he whispered to her. "This name they have given you. Can you tell me what it is?"

"No, my Lord. I do forgive your callousness, but in this new life I've been given I cannot permit that treasured part of myself to pass your ears, let alone be spoken with your voice. Even if I did, it is by my request a name a man would need lips to speak. I need never abide hearing it from you."

A tear escaped the corner of his eye and drew a line of hot flame down his temple. "Will you stay until after it is over?"

"Of course not, my Lord. You must know that."

He found that he did. "I'm sorry."

She kissed his wrist. "I know."

They fell into a silence that ended as Rhaij appeared, this time as naked as the rest of them, and so even more clearly a creature of those other skies s/he sometimes spoke about. A part of his/her body with no analogue on any human form Jin had ever seen hung enflamed, in a manner that testified to his/her own great excitement, and s/he said, "Jin: you do us honor with this passage. All of the human acolytes of this Temple, and all of us of the race that founded it, will watch your moment of transcendent bliss with envy and longing, taking inspiration from the courage you show in traveling where we all hope to follow."

He swallowed. "Thank you."

"Understanding what is about to happen to you is not fully necessary, but as it may enhance your experience to be able to follow what would otherwise be alien and incomprehensible, we leave you with this final, helpful explanation. What you are about to feel is the divine act of mating, as it is perceived by a soft and mindless creature that dwells among the stones of a shallow ocean, beneath suns so distant that none of their light has ever reached the heavens you know. It takes place over such an extended period of time that the egg-bearing participant who you would designate a female needs nourishment to avoid dying of starvation during the act; as a result, she devours the male, one tiny piece at a time, over the period necessary to achieve consummation. The gods of their sphere showed kindness and mercy in arranging that in exchange for this sacrifice on his part, she secretes a fluid that turns his agony to euphoria, his fear to joy, his very last moments before personal extinction to a sensation we can only describe as the most loving kiss of God. None of this will hurt you, Jin. As far as my people can determine, it is the purest expression of bliss in the entire universe."

He closed his eyes. "I understand."

Nuuij said, "Blessings to you. We will begin in just a few minutes."

S/he turned and exited the chamber through the arched doorway, leaving Jin alone with the woman no longer nameless, in a silence driven as much by memory as by anticipation.

His past lover's gentle touch did not leave his wrist. He remained aware of the warmth that passed from her fingers, to flesh that now felt so much colder than hers; and as the long minutes passed, and the wait for his life's greatest moment stretched, he opened his eyes again, and regarded her, half-expecting to find her veneer of compassion stripped away, and a true face of her loathing for him revealed with a clarity that would permit no more denials.

As it happened, she had turned away from him for a moment, and was unaware of his gaze. She was an edifice visible in profile, her golden skin aglow above a slight, melancholy smile. A solitary tear sat in the center of her cheek, its descent toward her jaw line arrested in place according to the common whim of such things; and in the center of that drop sat a single diamond-shaped mote of light, reflecting a candle burning somewhere in the chamber.

It reminded him of nothing so much as some distant star, warming the sky above earth too alien for him to walk.

A TABLEAU OF
THINGS THAT ARE

When they ordered me down off my pedestal, I had nowhere else to go.

Life as a statue is easy. They make you ascend the pedestal, turn you to stone, remove your ability to move, and leave you to watch the turn of the seasons in a world you cannot touch or care about, anymore. You can only stand in the public garden where all the convicted are placed, and you watch with dull and distant interest at the visitors who stroll past, living the lives of the quick, sometimes interested in all the immobile condemned, and sometimes not.

It is not fun, but it is not torture either, the way it would be if you were left the capacity to care. Fun is just a word that no longer applies, and the years are just time, crawling by like a snail on a pane of glass. It is easy because it requires no effort and takes nothing from you but your humanity.

Returning to the world, once you have served your sentence, is more difficult.

The custodians of the gardens don't give you any money and they don't offer you a job; they just say, "leave," and if you're smart, you start walking. You must, because otherwise they'll petrify you again and put you on another pedestal, frozen in whatever position they have chosen for you. This time you will remain there forever, and many have, because their dulled wits did not provide the impetus for the first step toward whatever destination a released stone man can choose.

I would not have been upset by permanent immobility. I was made of stone and did not care about anything. But after some delay to urge my thoughts back into constructive motion, I remembered that I'd once had a home; the place where I'd been when they'd come for me, where I'd lived as a short-tempered idiot and a married man, where I'd broken a man's back in a barroom fight, and earned my ten years on display as a statue.

I put one foot in front of the other, and then did it again, and after that did it again, a process that once begun, took care of itself. I did not even have to think of it. My legs, given the order to walk, obeyed, and left me alone with my thoughts, which were not many. What thoughts I had only accumulated like drifting sediment, and most of them were of a woman's name.

Ariella.

I made my way out of the park and from there out of the city and from there into the countryside, trudging past villages that did not make much fuss about me as long as I did not tarry or interfere with the lives of those still made of flesh. I sometimes saw people at their fences, watching me as I passed, their hands folded against their chests in silent judgment. I left them behind only to face a new set of pitiless eyes, bearing the same warning, at the next curve of the road, or the one after that.

Soon those populated places thinned out. I entered the places where I was most of the time the only being visible. The land became less dominated by farms and more dominated by woods and empty fields. I marched through torrential rain and the road became a soft strip of mud, where my stone shoes sank to ankle-depth, turning every step into an exercise in first freeing a foot from imprisonment. It got cold. Now the people I encountered wore heavy coats, and exhaled little clouds of vapor. Some coughed from chests clogged from winter illnesses, and they looked miserable, a state of being I vaguely envied, even though I was stone all the way through and had no lungs to clog. What cold I felt, the part that would always be part of me now that I was no longer flesh, was the chill that goes with being stone. But I remembered being a man and registered the winter through the way it looked, if not the way it felt against a body that was no longer flesh; the grayness of it, the sense winter tends to have that the world will never be warm again. It looked like I was peering inward at the thing I had become.

The entire journey had only two significant social interactions, before I reached the distant parish where I lived.

One was with a band of hooting boys, throwing rocks and snowballs, calling me a big dumb stupid rock and demanding to know what crime I had committed, that kind of thing. I said nothing, in part because it would have done no good and in part because I was still so unused to speech that my attempts sounded like an anvil being dragged across a slate. My most heartfelt reaction, the urge to seize one of the little bastards by the head and then make a fist, mashing every cruel impulse into a red paste, flashed in me, but took so much time to form that it outlasted my will. I just walked until they tired of me.

The other interaction I had was more significant. The cold snap had gone away, and I found another stone man lying on his back in an unkempt patch of yellow grass. He must have been there for some time, because he was half-buried by a recent snowfall which had turned to slush and filthy water in the hollows that form on the body of a supine man. I altered my course long enough to approach him, and stared down at the eyes that gazed unblinking at the gray sky. Like all stone men, he had the features of the being he'd been until convicted of whatever crime had sentenced him to petrification, and in all respects but the motionless cast to his face and the ageless pinpoints in his eyes he seemed to be the commemoration of a fresh-faced young man, untouched by the evils of the world.

I asked him if he was all right.

"I am stone," he said.

It had been a stupid question.

I asked him if he needed any help getting up.

"I will not be getting up," he replied.

I asked him if there was anyone who he wanted informed of his whereabouts.

"I think not," he said. "It has been many years. Everybody I loved must be dead. Why did they make you a statue?"

"I killed a man."

"Just one?"

He was downright chatty for a stone man.

"Yes."

"I killed two women. I was the kind of man who enjoyed doing things like that. When they petrified me, I stood in the garden for forty years, and my enjoyment of anything is gone."

I told him I was on my way to see the wife I had left behind.

He said, "Why?"

During none of this did he move as much as a twitch, and I thought about how little his existence had changed, since his days on public display. Maybe my existence would change more, when I found Ariella.

I abandoned him, and though it has been many years, I have no doubt that he is there still.

I continued my journey. I did not need to stop. I did not need to rest. I did not need food or water and I did not feel the strain of the long journey in my legs. I did not get tired. There were times when if I paid no attention to the testimony of my eyes, I could almost forget that I was not still on that pedestal, watching the years go by from inside a cage of immobility. There were other times when I considered not going home at all, but almost without realizing it I left the road and took a narrower path into the hills, into the forest of bare trees where I at long last found the old, rickety two-story home with the wraparound porch. It still stood, though it showed the passage of years, and it badly-needed a coat of paint. But there were clothes flapping on the line, and the sound of a singing woman drifted from the open window.

I almost climbed the porch stairs to knock on the front door, but before I could the front door opened and Ariella came out, dressed for housework and drying her hands with a rag. For a moment, her brow knitted in confusion, and for that moment I took a mental inventory on what the years had done to the woman I'd married. She had lighter brown hair streaked with gray and she'd given up on straightening it, allowing it to instead become its mop of curls, blowing in the wind. She had the beginnings of crow's feet and laugh-lines at the corners of her mouth. But her skin was still golden in the sun, and her eyes were still big and bright, and when she saw through the stone to the man I had been, her hand shot to her mouth, and she whispered my name, "Holt."

She did not look happy to see me. Why should she? The husband taken was not the husband returned. But after a moment's hesitation she came down the steps and approached, in something like apprehension, before rushing the rest of the distance to hurl her arms around me. "Holt," she said again, and "Holt," and when I failed to raise my arms to return the embrace, "Oh, Holt, my love. Look what they've done to you."

I knew I looked different, even allowing for the difference between flesh and stone. I did not wear quite the same face. I was stone and that meant I'd been weathered by ten years of rain and snow. My features had been smoothed of some of their lines. My body below had been protected, insofar as it could be, by the very clothes I'd been wearing when the keepers of the stone gallery spoke the words of transformation; and so above my stone form I wore a stone jacket, and stone trousers, and stone shoes, and they were all parts of me now, just like my exposed hands and wrists and face. I'd been wearing a brimmed hat before my petrification and had declined to take it off, presuming that it might protect my features from rain. But wind had found a way to drive the storms into my stone face, from time to time, and so it too showed the march of time; or so it had looked to me on my journey, when I found my reflection in glass windows, or in the puddles on the ground. It had to be shocking for her, as the mark time had made on her own still-beautiful face would have been shocking for me, had I been a man capable of seeing it in the way a man would.

I said, "It's good to see you," and I think she might have known that I only said it because it was something an absent husband should say, when he makes it back home after an absence of many years. But already I knew it was not. I could feel dull relief that she was alive and that she was well, but not the surging joy that should have come with seeing her again. She had become something I perceived at a distance, through a gray curtain that I could not part.

Then the door slammed again, and I saw that a man had left the house.

I did not know him, not at first. He was no familiar neighbor, no distant relative, just a bearded man with round shoulders, with unkempt crabgrass hair and a pair of dark eyebrows so thick that the eyes beneath them appeared to view the world through a thicket of weeds. It was bad now because of his scowl, matched with a grimace that displayed a thin sliver of tiny, yellow teeth. He was clearly not happy to see my intrusion this close to the woman who was once mine, and the bed that was now his. I should have felt equal outrage at his very presence, but the gray filter of my nature prevented the sight of him from rousing more than dull interest.

It made sense, I thought. What was Ariella supposed to have done, with her husband petrified for a stupid barroom killing? Create an empty space where once there was a person and soon enough something else must come along to fill it. To the degree that I could have an opinion on anything, I approved.

But that was before he opened his mouth.

He said, "As if this day wasn't already a big stinking pile of shit."

* * * *

Ariella introduced him to me as Defiance Cole, and he operated a small toolmaking shop in town, about five miles up the main road. Ariella specified that he was the grandson of Liberty Cole, who I did remember: a poisonous old bastard, ancient even when I was a child, who had once run the establishment in question. Liberty had been as taciturn while flesh as I now was in stone. Once upon a time, my father had accused him of hoarding conversation like it was made it of gold and only spending what amounted to pennies. I had never known that he had a wife, let alone descendants, and what Defiance said to me now would be a preview of the relationship to come.

"Fine. You came. Now get your murdering carcass away from here. You ain't welcome."

Still, there are two kinds of women married to men, those who obey and those that take charge, and Ariella had always been the one in charge. "We ain't married yet, De; this is still my land."

Then she took my hand, and I saw what happened to her eyes when she felt its cold, lifeless texture. "Long as you don't want no trouble, you can stay as long as you want."

Defiance said, "I going to have to put my foot down," and this was I suppose the key proof that I was no longer a man, because the stupid, troublemaking, brawling idiot I'd once been would have been wrestling him into the dirt by now.

She said, "Your foot don't mean nothing up or down."

"You cain't let him in the house. He'll crash right through the floorboards, and break everything he touches. I wouldn't even let him in the porch."

Ariella's eyes went angry at this, but she had to agree it was a reasonable boundary. "Okay."

I did not protest my need for shelter. I had spent ten years out in the open, immobile, the sport of both the frigid air of winter and the blazing heat of summer. I had been covered with snow and I had been the platform for fallen leaves. Pigeons had nested on my hat brim. I had felt none of it. But shelter was a feature of the life I'd known as man, and so I allowed Ariella to lead me behind the house, across the ragged grass of the field, and to the aging barn left over from that one golden summer in childhood, when my father had let me keep a horse.

That summer had been the last uncomplicated season of my life, the last time when anything had felt possible, when I had felt that I could have been anything. My later life with Ariella had been something else, adult happiness, which is always a defiant cry in the face of adult desperation.

I had told myself that the horse loved me, and it had seemed to, nuzzling my hand and lowering its great elongated head for attention. But then my father's debts had come due, and he had needed to trade the horse in exchange for forgiveness. I had screamed in his face that I hated him and for years I had until that hate was replaced with a coldness that never went away. Even as the life spark inside him started to flicker, and he became that seated presence who needed to be cared for and cozied, I had still been a preview of this man of stone, distant and unreachable. I had been annoyed at his neediness, and let him know it whenever I could. I'd been a bastard, and it was only after he was gone that it had occurred to me to feel bad about it. But I was past shame now. I was a stone man, and so I regarded the ruin as what it was, a rickety structure that remained upright out of sheer inertia. There were holes in the roof and walls that looked like they craved collapse, but I did not need much. Once in its shadow, I felt the vague distant satisfaction that was a ghost of the way of a man would feel, when he had walked a great distance and finally found shelter from the rain.

Ariella asked me if it would do and I said, "Yes," because there was no other thing I could say. Defiance warned again that I better stay out here and not try to enter the house, and I said, "Yes," for the same reason. Then she hugged me again and said we would talk soon, and left, the augurs of a loud argument forming in the space between her and the man she'd chosen as my replacement.

I did not weep. I did not attempt to follow. I did not sink to the dirt and bury my face in my hands.

I was stone.

As the clouds in the sky became streaked with purple, I heard the distant shouted voices. They were like almost all human conversations to me: muffled and irrelevant, a reminder of a connection I would never have again. Their content evaded me. I thought of the chair I'd broken over Mose Ferguson's back. The savage pleasure of that moment was also a feeling I could no longer summon. The voices carried on the wind and then eventually stopped, and I let concern go the same way as everything else.

* * * *

The night surrendered dominion over the world. The sun rose and climbed toward the sky, its passage visible via the shifting angle of the shafts of light admitted by the holes in the roof. I gave some thought to stepping outside where the sun's blessing fell everywhere and not just in scattered splinters, but I who had spent years at a time limited to whatever sights passed before my stone vision and had fallen out of the habit of shifting, even in the slightest, to choose a different vantage point.

In early morning Defiance showed up at the entrance to the barn and stood there for all of thirty seconds before storming off, in a hail of curses. Ariella arrived after noon wearing a white sun dress, with her hair tied back and fresh color applied to her cheeks. "Don't be lazy, Holt. Let's go for a walk."

I followed her, not saying much, as she told me what the years without me had been like, about the long lonely nights and the suitors who had not taken well to being told that she would wait for me. Ultimately, she apologized, "I waited as long as I could." And then she told me about how the men had stopped calling on her: except, when she thought that part of her life was done, cold practical Defiance, who had presented his case not in romantic terms but instead as an exercise in pooling resources.

"He's never said he loved me," she said, a clear invitation for me to say that I still did. "But he's never been cruel."

A brook passed through the woods a short walk away, pooling around a boulder that sat in the center of the water, forever unmoved by the pooling at its base. It had been one of the sacred places of our time together, and it was by the dappled light of its rushing waters, that she laid out a comfortable old blanket, and began placing food taken from her pantry.

"A picnic," she explained.

I did not point out that as a stone man I had no possible use for, and therefore no interest in, food. I understood that some rituals must be respected even when they no longer had any meaning. So, I sat cross-legged on my side of the blanket, hands planted on knees, while she bit into an apple and told me how good it tasted. I could recall any number of past afternoons when in idylls stolen from the hours when I had to haul goods and she had to labor as a seamstress to support ourselves, we curled up on this very spot and pretended for a few minutes that it was Eden and that we never had to return to the demands of the world again.

I think she wanted me to respond as a man. But she had to know that even if I could access a part of me once made of flesh, using it in any real way would have injured her. It was another gulf between what I'd once been able to have and what I would now never have again, and it almost kept me from noticing that as she spoke about the joys of the past, only some of what she said was true. All the bad parts, and with me there had been plenty of bad parts, she omitted; all the good parts she inflated with air and invested with a gravity that made the life of two people like a grand idyll the world would never know again.

One thing was certain. Whatever she remembered that had been so grand, her current life with the scowling, ungenerous Defiance suffered from the comparison. She kept apologizing for various things he had done, and saying, "But he's a good man."

It was possible to believe Defiance a good man. It was not possible, I thought, to believe me one. I had loved her as best I could, but a stone man is forced to face the whole truth and I could know, from the perspective of a creature incapable of self-loathing, that I had not loved her well.

After a spell she fell into a silence almost as deep as mine, one that held us both as the brook made its bubbling noises a few short steps from us. Then she said, "This don't do nothing for you, does it?"

I thought about it and gave her an answer as close to the truth as I could get, which was that the man I'd been was cursed to sleeping in his blanket of stone, and could not wake. But as tears sprung to her eyes, I also said that if the past meant nothing I would not have come so far to return. I would not have joined her at this picnic with the food I could not eat and the cold brook water that would not provide comfort to my naked toes. I stopped talking before telling her that if being with her made me at all happier, it was something I experienced only as a certain lessening of the weight that pulled me down with every step.

Her eyes flared. "You're the one who destroyed it all. You know that. You had to do what you did, because you had to break this like you done everything else."

"It's true," I told her.

The man I'd been would have followed that up with a string of self-serving excuses, gradually returning the blame to her, but the man of stone could only acknowledge the absolute truth.

She returned me to my barn and thanked me for the pleasant afternoon before abandoning me to the deepening shadows. I knew she would come back tomorrow and perhaps the day after, but would soon come to reason that it hurt too much to see me again. Before long she would skip days at a time, and then perhaps not long after that it would be weeks. One day she would startle with the realization that she had spent a snowy month not venturing as far as my new home, and she would rush to find me, still standing in the same place where she'd last left me, and my calm equanimity would suddenly make her hate me, would leave her pounding on my chest with anger at her own stupidity at letting me reside here. That was the only way it could go, and I knew this with the cold certainty that could only come with being a man of stone.

The night came and I stood throughout it, not moving.

And in the morning it was not Ariella who came to me, but Defiance.

* * * *

He stared at me the way he had the prior morning, and after extended silence said, "So you're really a pathetic son of a bitch, ain't you? Stone or flesh, both."

I did not respond.

"She never stops talking about you. Not after we got together and not now that you're back. Still. Not only the good things. About how you drank and how you wandered off whenever life seemed too hard. How you had no patience for nothing but drinking and fighting. But also, how kind you was. She won't stop talking about how kind you was, and how her heart broke when they took you away. Seems to me it's the story of a piece of trash who wouldn't stay home and take care of his woman, one who's so selfish he came back as a stone man, to hurt her still."

I did not respond.

He told me that he and Ariella had made love the previous night. He did not use the phrase, "made love." He used the ugliest word anyone can, rendered uglier by the worst way anyone could say it, with a leer. He said it as if with that word he was not reliving the memory of entering her but making it an exercise in violating me through her, like a bullying dog will sometimes mount a weaker one just to make the point.

"She didn't want to. She was in no fit mood, not after trying to get some decent conversation, or whatever, out of you. She'd been crying, and crying hard, and trying to pretend she wasn't, and the last thing she wanted to do, once that stopped, was doing her duty by me. I didn't force her. I want you to know that. I never had to physically force no woman. I ain't the type. But she done it anyway, just to make peace with me, just to keep me happy 'cause she now knows I'm all I got. She ain't ever loved it with me, I can tell, but she always done that long as we been together, because that's the price. And maybe it's true that she makes it okay by thinking of you, but I want you to know that from now on it'll help me to think of your worthless ass out here in the barn, thinking about what you threw away." When I still said nothing he showed teeth the yellow of pus and he said, "I would prob'ly kill myself if I was you, if that was even possible."

He said all this while keeping his distance, trusting in his legs to carry him faster than mine could carry me. But I did not lunge and after a few seconds he grinned with renewed nastiness.

What he did then was unlatch the hook that sealed the flap of his trousers, pull out his man-root, and baptize me with a glittering stream of his bottomless contempt.

I did nothing to stop him, and why should I? As a statue I'd known similar insults from more birds that could count. I'd been caked with the stinking white of their droppings, and had the fossilized turds colonize my shoulders and the brim of my stone hat, feeling nothing until the rain and wind washed the filth away, and left me clean enough for more birds to sully. It had been nothing personal to the birds. It was everything personal to Defiance. And while it occurred to me that maybe I should cup his face in one stone palm and pierce his eyes with pointing finger and pinky, it was a fleeting spark that failed to catch fire. I let him enjoy his piss.

When he was done, I told him, "I'm not a statue."

"Yeah?" he said. "Why don't you do something to stop me?"

I did not respond.

He waited, but if Ariella could not get more than a few words at a time from me, then neither could he, and after a minute or so he decided that this was satisfactory, and left.

Until the next morning, when he came back, and pissed on me again.

● ● ● ●

Ariella took me on three more picnics that week, two more in the following week, and one more in the week after that; and after that, they were irregular events, sometimes daily for as long as a week and then, as I'd predicted, sometimes not at all for as long as a month.

Sometimes she had some chore for me, like the time a windstorm left a tall tree partially uprooted and teetering in the direction of the house. It made sense for her to fetch me and have the helpful stone man use his superior strength to wrestle the trunk into some position that endangered nothing but other trees. After that and other necessary feats of strength she thanked me as sweetly as she could, but when this failed to warm me she averted her eyes, and I returned to my barn, to stand on the same spot I'd left, in what had become a little worn place, the opposite of a pedestal.

Defiance's hate was much more faithful than the remains of her love.

He kept coming, kept baptizing me with each first morning piss, kept me apprised of the latest developments in his physical relationship with my wife. He told me when she claimed to enjoy it and when she did not. He took special joy in telling me of the times he woke her out of a deep sleep, in the wee hours when the view out their window displayed only a black void, when she resisted and he insisted and she ultimately agreed to take care of him, before she could reward her exhaustion with sleep. He used the word "dutiful" to describe these occasions, to underline that she acquiesced out of obedience, not passion. And then he said, "Maybe you could do better, if you could reach yours. But it's under those clothes of your'n, ain't it? It's got a real tight stone blanket, don't it? Why don't you try chiseling it out. I'll wait."

I did not respond.

Live ten years as a statue and you learn that hours change when you have no way of filling them. Live as a man and time is a parade of events, some joyous and some upsetting and some impossible to fathom. You mark the days by the things that mark them, like the day you tell your father you hate him or the day your eye is blackened by someone you picked a fight with or the glorious moment when somebody better than yourself first says she loves you. Remove those markers and all of time fuses. Pass by a waterfall and it is a moment. Stop briefly and it becomes a place. Stand there forever and it is no longer a temporary phenomenon, but a feature, the water that has been falling forever, and will be falling forever. To a stone man the sun is no longer a glowing thing that crosses the sky and changes night into day, and disappears to allow night's return, but an eternal and incessant shutter, that never changes and never makes a difference. So it was with the drama of Ariella and Defiance, and the many months I spent in the barn, bathed in the changing light without ever being touched by it. Her hurt and his abuse became eternal, and I felt them recede from me, like the movement of clouds as seen from the bottom of a deep well. They had nothing to do with me. Her hurt had nothing to do with me; his cruelty had nothing to do with me. I was stone, and if I was not content then at least I also did not want.

Then one morning Ariella showed up at the opening of the barn. Her hair was longer than it had been the last time I'd seen her, and duller, as if she hadn't washed or brushed it for a while. There were tear tracks on her cheeks, and red blotches on her nose. She stared at me for a while, her chest heaving with hoarse breath, and said, "Direct question. Can you even say you love me?"

I replied, "Yes."

"Just to pretend?"

"Yes."

"Say it, then. Say it whether you mean it or not."

"I love you."

It sounded like a rote line from one of the prayers that come at the end of a long and tedious church season, at the point when everyone is exhausted and eager for the freedom of a warm afternoon. It did not ring with sincerity.

Ariella heard it and she covered her eyes and when she removed her hand her gaze was hard, filled with the fire that went with trying to force herself to hate me. "Now say it like you mean it."

"I can't."

"*Do* you love me?"

"I'm a stone man."

"Damn you," she said, and I did not see her again that year.

Not long after that, the snow fell in a blanket that collapsed another part of the roof, covering the dirt below with a snowdrift as high as my knees.

There were bad storms that winter, with raging winds that made my walls shake, that drove the small creatures of the wood to seek shelter alongside me. I began to notice the regular visitation of a black rat that sometimes paused at my feet and looked up at my face, its whiskers trembling. It was never with me for more than a few minutes, but in those few minutes it seemed to know that the stone giant it saw was not some strangely shaped rock but a living and thinking being as capable of seeing it as it was of seeing me. It grew fascinated. Like some of the pigeons and the squirrels of the park where I'd spent all those years as a statue, it became a regular acquaintance, not a friend because I could not be stirred to that condition, but nevertheless a thing that could communicate a shallow, default *So there you are*, that I was able to answer with the identical thought. *So there you are*, I thought, and it changed nothing at all, but at least it was a thought, a moment of punctuation that interrupted the silence.

And then one day I happened to be watching when a barn owl swooped down and eviscerated it with its talons, and where a man might have felt grief, I felt only the shifting of the Earth.

The winter passed. The snow melted. I thought that I would grow moss, lose definition, and become one of those ancient monuments human beings encounter once in a while, that look they might have once been a sculpture of a specific man, but are now so worn that they have lost all their features and are just vague suggestions of the identity they'd once worn.

I thought of making love to Ariella. I thought of the times we had to get up in the morning but delayed the day by a few minutes, to exercise our passions and laugh in each other's arms. I thought of how sometimes we got silly and could not stop laughing. I thought of what it had felt like when she kissed my eyes, and they were just little visitations of memory, not attached to any identifiable feeling, no more beloved or mourned than the time I dropped a heavy stone on my foot and spent the summer with a limp. They had the same value, these two memories, and I could not give one more force than the other. They just were. And yet I thought of the lovemaking more, trying to coax feeling from it; and yet I struggled to answer her question, why I'd been so driven to come back.

Then one early evening in spring Defiance came to the barn, his gait uncertain, his eyes unfocused and his abuse of me slurred, and he laughed long and hard and said, "I bet you never even got cold, did you? Answer me, you great big gray idiot. Did you get cold?"

I answered honestly. "I'm a stone man."

"You don't feel nothing at all, do you? Not the snow, not the rain, not the summer days when it's so hot a proper man can hardly draw a breath. Ain't nothing good or bad to you, not even the slightest bit. It just is."

"Yes."

"Let's see about that," he said, and he wound up and struck me in the side of the face with a claw hammer.

I was stone. It did not hurt. I felt the impact, though, and I felt an infinitesimal piece of that cheek chip off and fall to my feet. I did not bat him away with a backhanded slap that would have left liquefied brain matter spilling out through his ears. I didn't even turn my head, to make eye contact and maybe terrify him into backing off. Time was a state of being. I waited for whatever blow came next.

None arrived. Instead, he dropped the hammer at my feet and screamed in my face from a distance of inches. His eyes were wet. He was bereft.

"I had something," he said. "That's what sticks with me. I *had* something. I had the best woman there ever was. I never thought I would but then she said yes and then I did. And you had to come back and give her dreams that couldn't be. Now it's all gone bad. Why couldn't you just do the decent thing and die?"

I said, "I'm not alive."

He did not piss on me that day. He just stumbled off, leaving the hammer, which remained at my feet in more or less the spot that had been the habitual place of my friend the black rat. In some ways the hammer turned out to be a truer friend. It did not wander off to conduct the necessary business of being alive. It did not disappear for hours or days at a time, and it did not get itself eaten by an owl. It stayed, and from time to time it occurred to me to take special notice of its presence, and think, *So. There you are.*

I heard more and more shouting from the house.

· · · ·

I do not know how long it was before Ariella came to visit again, this time favoring one leg and with a fresh shock of gray hair along one side of her face. She'd lost weight and was not emaciated, but was paler, more drawn. There was a swollen purple place along the side of her jaw.

Her gaze fell toward the claw hammer before rising again, to meet mine.

She said, "You didn't come back for me, not even the slightest bit."

"No."

"How come? And don't tell me it's because you're a stone man."

Though I might have told her that it had never been anything but ridiculous to imagine my cold lips kissing her warm ones, and more ridiculous still to imagine me holding her in my unyielding arms, these were sentences beyond my ability to feel, let alone speak. "I'm not a man of flesh."

"You could kill him for me. I know you're strong enough. Don't you want to?"

"No."

"Even if he hits me?"

"No."

"Don't you hate him for it?"

"I'm a stone man."

She knelt at my feet, weeping, and I said not a word to comfort her, because I had no words to comfort her or heart to even want to comfort her. I remembered what it had been like to be beside her when we were both human beings and her emotions had grown as stormy as a tempest-tossed sea. We had fought hard, during our years together, because of the differences between what I was and what she wanted, differences that I suppose must always exist between lovers, when they have actual blood running through their veins. I had sometimes, but not always, known what to say in those days.

After a while we both heard the distant sound of Defiance calling in anger. She rose, wiped her nose with the back of her hand, and left without looking back, to attend his call.

In what remained of her life, she would return to me only once more, and when that happened, she would speak not a word.

• • • •

Defiance showed up more often than that. It wasn't every day. But on mornings several days apart, there were three or four of his urinary baptisms, accompanied by the usual mockery, though he'd lost the taste for that. He had to know by now that a man of stone could not be bruised by words, barbed or otherwise. There was no name he could call me that would get past my shell, no word-image he could paint about his treatment of Ariella that would infuriate me enough to get me to throw a deadly punch.

Then one morning he showed up with a sledgehammer.

The smaller hammer had chipped me. The sledgehammer was heavier, meant for breaking large rocks into smaller ones. The first time it flew, half of my right hand turned to powder. He stumbled backward, both horrified by this and oddly thrilled by it. He asked me if it hurt. I told him no. He wound up again and struck my lower arm, scattering rock chips and inflicting a hairline crack from my elbow to my wrist. He laughed at this but didn't swing the sledge again, in part because he was breathing like a man who had just run ten miles but also because he could do the math and could see that if he devoted a day to my deconstruction he could reduce me to gravel in a matter of hours, leaving himself with no other form of satisfaction. He vomited, left the sledgehammer at my feet, and stumbled off, promising to return the next morning.

All day the sun crawled across the sky. Then it set, and at night the constellations rose and traversed their own path.

Defiance returned the next day, and the day after that, and the day after that, each day doing what damage he could do in a swing or three, before once again dropping the sledge and storming off, with a promise to return.

Did it hurt when pieces of me crumbled? Not in the sense that flesh hurts. Was it horrifying? Not in a sense that afflicts a soldier, staring aghast at his own severed limb. A man can die from the loss of blood and a man can go mad at the sight of part of himself, now ripped asunder and left as fodder for scavengers. A stone man, I discovered, cannot. There is pain, of a sort. It does not rise to the level of agony. But it was still the knowledge that part of myself had been ripped away, and it was still a violation, and if it did not lead to gnashing and wailing it was still sadness, still the awareness that everything I was had been diminished yet again.

I would never again pick up anything with that arm, which within a week was a splintered stump severed above the elbow. But what did I need to pick up, really? What had I, that was worth the effort of handling? What self did I have, that was worth defending? And if I felt pain, in what way was it preferable to feel nothing? I suppose some stone men other than myself would have cared to do what it sometimes occurred to me I should do, fight back, and do to Defiance's limbs what he had done to mine, but again, it all felt so distant that it was not worth bothering. So I just allowed him to take my arms and to leave a giant crater in my chest and to rip a chunk out of my hip as he took my arms. I did nothing as he told me every day that the next day he would take more; as he promised that sooner or later I would just be a head, to bury in some place in the forest where she would no longer be able to find me.

So it went, until the very last time I saw the woman I had once been able to love.

It was a moonlit night. I heard her coming down the path from the house and I saw her stop in the open barn door. The light played on her silvery hair, now marked by a fist-sized bare spot that glistened in the darkness. Blood glistened on her lower lip. She looked at me and she looked at the scattered ruins at my feet. When she saw what had been done to me her right hand rose to her lips.

"Leave him," I told her. "Go as far as you can. Save yourself while you can."

She said nothing. Just dashed to my feet and ran away again, the soft thud of her footsteps fading in the darkness.

* * * *

Time may mean nothing to a stone man, but that doesn't mean that we can't be aware of it, not if we have reason to be aware of it.

When I was displayed as a statue, I saw no particular reason to keep track of the years. I was aware that they were turning, but I did not keep count.

As the armless statue in the barn, I did have some reason to wonder and so I counted the winters as they passed. Whenever the first snows came after the long summers, I added a mental entry in my internal calendar.

This is how I knew that two years had passed when the air around me turned to thick smoke, blowing from the direction of the house. This is how I knew that seven years had passed when time claimed what was left of the roof. This is how I knew that twelve years had passed when a stray dog birthed its puppies in a shelter of collapsed roof, and when the four of them emerged from the haven of their days as blind helplessness to gambol round my unmoving ankles as if I was the territory they had to win. That was how I knew that fourteen years had passed when a gray-bearded vagabond unknown to me chose to pitch his tent just outside what had once been the home of a child's horse, and for three months used me as the helpless but unprotesting target of his conversation, all while calling me Julia. This is how I knew that seventeen years had passed the day a storm of historic proportions passed by, and the rain did not stop for eight days.

This is how I knew that twenty-two years had passed when I received the last of the visitors to the barn.

She came walking down the hill that had once led up to a house where over the years two men had found different ways to hurt a good woman.

She entered the space that could no longer be quite said housed a barn, and she studied me from what had been the threshold, waiting for me to say something.

She was made of stone, of course. On that last night she had taken the claw hammer with her, and it had not escaped me what she intended for it. She had done it even though she knew the penalty that she would surely suffer, for such a heinous crime; even though it would have been easy to get away with it, had she made any effort to bury Defiance in the woods and tell the authorities that he had run off.

"I confessed," she told me, in lieu of a hello, and I understood at once that it was the only thing she could have done, to become a stone woman whose long hair was a solid curtain around her cheeks, and whose knee-length skirt was now like a cliff face, descending from her waist.

She was not the living woman I'd known. As I've noted, that one was gone; was dead, really. What stood now was something else, something I was now meeting for the first time.

I said, "They gave you a longer sentence than they gave me. More than twenty years."

She said, "You broke a chair over the back of a man who was trying to hurt you. I crept up on a man as he slept. You were sorry about what you'd done. I showed no remorse. Mine was a worse crime. It was a wonder they didn't give me fifty."

I was impressed by the long speech, which had gone on for some time, by the standards of the stone.

I asked, "Why didn't they?"

"The sculpture garden was getting too crowded. People of flesh are always hurting each other. They needed to let some of us go, to make room for the next."

I had no hand for her to take. Both my arms were still rubble at my feet. But she gestured for me to join her and this I did, walking at her side as she took me down the familiar and overgrown path to our favorite spot, on the shores of that brook. On the way she told me that the house in which she and I had lived was not only a blackened shell, having burned to the ground on, I presumed, the day of the thick smoke. It must have been some time, she said, because there were now two trees growing out of it. Someday soon, she said, it would be impossible to tell that there had ever been a house there at all, and I said nothing, because there was nothing I could do with this information.

Then we reached our imagined Eden, and she told me what we had to do.

I obeyed, wading into the creek water and making my way to that boulder which rose above the waters, like a miniature continent that had yet to be settled. I had no arms to climb with, but she had arms strong enough to lift me, and she used all that strength to grasp me by my hips and slide me upward until my weight lay balanced on the summit. Undignified it may have been. But what is dignity?

Then she splashed around to the other side of the boulder and used her intact limbs to ascend. She was as graceful as stone as she'd been in life, and it was more like hopping up, than climbing. Once she was standing above me, she took me under my foreshortened arms and helped lift me to my feet. Even without my arms I would not have known how to embrace her, as it had been many years and my human knowledge of such things had atrophied to almost nothing. But she slipped her intact arms around my waist and pulled me to her, until there was not the width of a finger between her lips and mine. It demanded response. I could not embrace her back, but I could lift my cracked stumps until they each touched her upper arms, and I could meet her eyes from a little height, and look on her with a nearness to another being that I had not experienced since my days as a man.

This was not a triumph of love. There was still no deep emotion and still no surge of passion. Even affection, the way men and women of flesh know it, was lost to us, and would never come again. But it was almost as a woman, so close to that state that it almost failed to matter, that Ariella peered back at me and said, "If you're wondering how I saw fit to forgive you, you can stop. I didn't."

"I know."

"But I'm stone too. I can't feel angry at you anymore. And this is where I've come to rest, the last place where I knew how to be happy. If you want, we can rest together."

"Good," I agreed.

We studied each other for a little bit, then brushed lips and by mutual unspoken agreement froze in place. We remained fixed at that moment, beneath the sun and the stars and above the sound of bubbling water, determined to stay until that brook ground both the pedestal and the lovers who stood there first to gravel and then to dust. It has been many, many summers and winters since that moment, and the boulder still stands, though we both sense that it might be narrower at its base. Collapse does not feel imminent, except in the sense that all things are, to those made of stone, tomorrow's sunrise being just as far away to us as the very end of the world.

Until then, time has done what time does. It has passed, but it has ceased being a parade of things that happen, and returned to what we know it always was, a tableau of things that are.